Adventures of
Scar and Floyd

WRATH OF MONTORIOUS

FREDERICK ALEXANDER

PAGE PUBLISHING, INC.
Conneaut Lake, PA

First originally published by Page Publishing 2021

ISBN 978-1-6624-2708-4 (pbk)
ISBN 978-1-6624-2709-1 (digital)

Printed in the United States of America

CHAPTER 1

My Unexpected Journey

Prologue

J ourney into this dystopian world, learning the roots of the hidden secrets from the past and face adversity with the characters. Do you long for something more in life? A place you can escape to and start over. Where no one knows you, but evil rules supreme? It has swarmed the lands of the peasants of this world. Don't be deceived to think that anything is a surprise. This place was always here. You were just looking in the wrong places, having blinders upon your eyes. Like rats when they rush to their next meal that has been infused with poison with their horde of brethren, not knowing it'll be they're last. Can you bear the pain of what lies ahead in this story? Or will you folly?

Do we make up our own view of life to hide behind how we really feel? That's how Scar felt. It all began one day when he was simply relaxing on a beach, soaking in the intense rays of the sun. He closed his eyes to hear the roar of the ocean and the waves that came in incessantly. Life was good. Or so he thought. What he didn't perceive that his life was about to change forever. Let me back up a bit to when he was just in his cozy home. Awakening to the sound of loud cars outside, birds singing tunes. His loud tenants above with their loud wild party. Scar was an inventor who loved to travel, eat, and enjoy life. He arose out of his bed, slipping on his slippers. Making his way to his workshop, for he was building something. Opening the door, proceeding in. Beginning to work meticulously on this necessary task. Everyone thought he was foolish to try and create such a thing, for it could not be done. He'd lost friends, thinking he became obsessed. So he enjoyed his solitude, working every day in his shop on his device that one day would be a very handy machine. "It's finished!" Scar yelled aloud. Picking up the device, he rushed out the door and began packing some things. Changed his clothes, making his way to the door of his apartment, Scar opened the door, racing down the hall. *Wham*! He'd ran into Mr. Benson. The two fell down on the floor.

"Will you get off me, boy?"

"I'm sorry, Mr. Benson."

Scar quickly got up and helped him to his feet. Then tried to run past the man.

"What are you in a hurry for anyway?"

"I've done it! I've finished it."

The man just laughed. "Sure. Sure, and I'm getting younger each day, right? Son, you've been working on that for years, and it's failed before. How do you know it'll work now?"

The two just looked at each other for a moment. He then stepped aside smiling. "Well, go on then."

Scar smiled back. Taking down the hall to a door that he swung open that led to a stairway. Racing up the stairs that led to the roof. He reached a door and opened it wide and ran to the middle of the roof. Scar pulled out his device and pressed a button. Many holograms popped out into the air. "Yes!" Scar shouted, he then scanned them to see what he wanted. Then aiming the device to an open spot above the huge roof, he pressed the button. The device shone bright making a funny noise, then a huge plane appeared. Scar almost fell to his knees. He walked to the door of the plane, opened it, got in, and threw his bag in the seat next to him, then slammed the door. Smiling, he started the engine. Scar steered the plane, picking up speed, he was almost to the edge. He was off soaring over buildings and houses. What Scar hadn't realized was that Mr. Benson was watching him from his window and saw him take flight. "Well done, kid," he said smiling, then pulled back the curtain. He flew up higher over the clouds. Flying for a good few hours, Scar grew tired and so he put the plane on autopilot. Later, he was awoken by a loud noise. He had entered a bizarre storm! Taking hold of the wheel, he fought to find a way out of it. Up ahead, he saw an island. Scar lowered the plane, nose down with fierce. Lighting struck the plane's wing. He and it skidded aggressively across the water brushing up against the shore. Scar opened the door, then looked around upon the beautiful scenery. Carrying a beach chair in one hand and his bag in the other, he splashed through the water, walking to a spot under a palm tree that had what looked like tasty coconuts. He climbed up the high tree and grabbed one, then dropped it in the sand. Sliding back down, he laid out on his chair, took a knife, and pierced a hole on the top of the coconut, poked a straw through, and began to drink.

Suddenly, the ground started to shake. This made Scar drop his drink. He was so startled. Looking around now to see if he could spot what had caused this massive shake. But there was nothing he could see, so Scar laid back in his chair resting his eyes. This time, he heard a funny noise come from the ocean, like something was emerging from the water. But Scar paid no mind but drifted off to sleep for a few seconds. He began to smell a repugnant smell, a strong aroma, a concoction of seaweed and raw fish. It was so unbearable that Scar began to cough and fell off his beach chair onto his knees. A glob of slobber fell on his head. "*Yuck!*" Scar tried to wipe off muck from his head and clothes. Having no luck, it just stuck to his hand. He looked down and opened his fingers, while some discolored muck dripped off. He casually looked up slowly. His eyes widened, a huge unusual shape shadowed above him. Standing above him was an enormous oversize crab. With pinchers the size of wrecking balls that lunged at him, he quickly dived out of the way as sand exploded up into the air like a mine had gone off. He lunged for his remote that had fallen out his pocket. "*No!* Why isn't it working?" said Scar. The crab drew closer. It surprisingly spoke.

"Yum!" said the crab.

"How is this possible?" said Scar, intrigued.

"It doesn't matter." The crab's mouth dripped even more drool as he talked. "You feeble people better pay up! He's coming!" The crab had an evil expression upon his face.

"What? Who?" asked Scar.

"You'll know soon enough, you incompetent little man" The crab laughed as he looked at Scar with his beady black eyes at what Scar was holding. "You can't hurt me with some puny device."

Scar ignored his remark and pressed down on a button again. "Yes!" A hologram appeared of numerous things. Scar pulled out what he desired, and it rapidly expanded into what he chose. A sword appeared instantly. The crab swatted Scar against a rock, making him drop his sword. He struggled to reach it. The crab drew closer. "Impressive device, but it will not save you. You will die before you can use it again!" The grotesque-looking creature charged him. Scar yelled as he stretched harder to grasp the sword, still no success. The giant crab was almost upon him snarling with his huge pinchers snapping, stomping, and creating massive craters in his place. Scar yelled as he reached out his arm again a bit more. Finally, success. He grasped the sword, rising to his feet, charging the oversize sea creature. He swung wildly at him, luckily slicing off a limb. The beast cried out. The two fought tremendously. Scar then sliced off another limb. He cursed as blood and water poured from his wound. "You will pay dearly for that." Scar retreated and ran into the jungle to prepare for the final battle. Splashing through mud and running through cobwebs. Scar became livid. "Blah! Yuck." He spat out cobwebs that stuck to his lip, then looked at his shoes. "Not my good clothes!" Scar looked at his shirt, examining the horrid damage to it. Then looked up at the sky, raising both hands into the air. "Im just on vacation! Why is this happening to me?" said Scar in disappointment. He took a deep breath as he looked ahead and spotted what he was searching for. Scar rushed through the jungle, coming to a waterfall that had a drop-off point. "Perfect," said Scar. Trees went tumbling down like dominoes. Loud roaring in the jungle was heard. Gulr! The monster rampaged through the jungle cursing. "I'll find you! I can smell you, boy!" He laughed. Scar turned and faced the jungle. Gripping his sword with two hands ready, waiting. He burst out of the jungle. Covered in tree branches, mud, and other gross stuff with dried-up blood near his wounds. Breathing heavily.

"Are you ready?" asked the beast. Scar looked down briefly, then back up at the creature and smirked.

"Are you? But I have one question," said Scar. The creature took a huge breath, growing impatient.

"Fine, you're going to die anyway," said the monster.

"Why are you here?" The crab then gave Scar a look as if he had no idea.

"Because, boy, it's time. We're all coming out of hiding, for the end of your world has come."

"What all of you? There's more of you? I don't understand"

The crab then roared, "Enough talk. I grow tired of you!" He charged Scar once more. Scar did the same—yelling, holding his sword. Soon as the two almost impacted, he slid under his body. Thankfully, the ground was slippery. He tried clamping him but just crushed a rock into bits and pieces. "Argh!" he collapsed in pain as he trembled to stand up. His insides poured out tiny bits of crawfish, water, and guts.

Then began to shake and fell over onto its back. He put his sword to his neck.

"Who created you?"

"I don't answer to vermin like you!" As the words were still coming out, Scar pressed his sword deep into his wound where his leg used to be. "*Argh!*" the crab yelled. "Okay. Okay, I'll talk! Dr. Montorious!"

Scar looked puzzled for a moment and yelled, "Hey, buddy! Who's this Dr. Montorious!?" The beast laughed.

"He's the end, the one who will rule this world."

"Not if I have anything to say about it." The monster just laughed again now, coughing in pain as he lay slowly dying.

"He's not to be challenged. He has an Army, thousands of loyal creatures he's created, even your kind is joining him."

"Where is this Dr. Montorious?" Scar asked. But before the crab could respond, he shriveled up and slowly decayed.

Scar fell to the ground in awe, staring now at the corpse. "I must find him and stop him, but I have no Army. People will think I'm crazy, more than they do now. I must not be in my world anymore." He had a plan to search this jungle to find people that would help him assist in taking this evil of a man down. But first, he needed to rest. He walked back into the jungle. Slicing through vines and webs. It seemed endless. "Whew!" said Scar. "I think it's time to turn in and rest." Looking for places to sleep, Scar pulled out his remote and pressed a button. A hologram appeared. He pulled out climbing gear, then walked a bit more, then looked up at a tall tree.

"*Ah*, here's a good spot!" He began to climb using the clamps that dug into the tree. "Don't look down. Don't look down," said Scar repeatedly to himself. "*Ow*!" Scar yelled as a berry hit him in the face. Scar looked up briefly rubbing his forehead. There was a baby monkey with big eyes. He kept his gaze on him as the monkey threw another medium-sized berry right at his eye. "Why, you little rat! Come here!" Scar tried to grab the little pest but lost his grip.

"*Ah!*" He fell down into a bush. Scar got up, mumbling to himself but heard a voice yell down, "This is my house!" He ignored his remark and used his clamps to climb back up. Finally getting up to his destination, he began to rest and drift off into a deep sleep. Hours had past, and it was nearly the next morning. Scar yawned and rubbed his eyes. "What the—" He opened his eyes fully to see that he was surrounded by little monkeys, and the annoying one was sitting on Scar's belly. "Will you get outta here?" He reached for his remote to pull out a weapon. All the little fury critters dispersed. "Yeah, that's what I thought." But little did Scar know, he was being watched by something, something that was very hungry. Making his way back down the tree, when a tremendous storm broke out suddenly. "Oh, great," said Scar, as he began yet again chopping down vines and swatting down cobwebs, muttering things to himself. The storm grew heavier, and the ground became marshy, making walking hard to do. "I hate this jungle!" Scar yelled as he yanked his foot out of the mud but lost balance and fell, starting to slide down a mudslide now. He relentlessly tried grabbing hold upon anything he could to save himself. Sliding faster now whizzing past trees. Scar looked up ahead and saw a drop-off point.

Using all his strength now to grasp ahold of something to save him, but it was too late. Landing facedown, disoriented. Little did he know that his remote had fallen out his pocket. "Oh." Scar touched his head as he looked around knowing his situation had gotten worse. Surrounding him were giant mudholes. Birds flew through the air chirping loudly. Something was coming. Creepy noises were in the distance that would have given your spine a shiver. Hurrying now into his pocket to find his remote was missing, Scar tried not to panic. Quickly getting up and began to search but had no luck.

The noises of what was approaching became louder now, and a chill ran down Scar's back as he saw only the eyes of this creature looking back at him from afar, keeping its gaze, studying him. It had bright-yellow eyes that then split and became snakelike. They were black in the middle. Scar slowly shifted his eyes to the ground and saw his device, just a few feet from his body from which he stood near a sinkhole. "I can make it," he said to himself, slowly inching over to his device but keeping his eyes upon the beast, which began to growl so intensely that he felt the ground shake. Still edging for his device, he finally picked it up. Another beast just like it sprouted out of the trees behind Scar. It was enormous, having a panther-shaped face with huge muscular legs and bearlike paws wielding a long tail that had a long needle at the end. The other monster came out of hiding.

He picked up his device and quickly pushed a button. He aimed it toward himself. It flashed a bright-green light. Scar was now wearing full armor that covered his face and body. Yielding two swords on his back, a crossbow with many arrows. He was ready. "You must be friends of that crab thing, eh?" The creatures laughed, glaring him down.

He removed both swords from his back and made a battle pose. One of the beasts lunged at him, but he dived out the way and jumped into the air and slashed its back but forgot about its tail as it tried to pierce his leg but only dented the armor. The next monster roared, charging him, managing to bite Scar. His mouth had a very strong grip. He held him in his mouth, then threw him. Suddenly, one of the creatures stood up on his hind legs like a man. His throat began to turn bright orange and red. A huge fireball formed aimed at Scar. His eyes grew big while he was lying on the ground. The fireball came at high speed toward him. Scar quickly rolled out of the way. It hit the tree decimating it.

Scar put away his swords. Pulling out his crossbow, he shot it in the beast's belly, making it angry. It charged him. He shot out numerous arrows to bring the monster down. It growled and bared its teeth. Arrows whizzed paced again. But it still charged, covered in arrows. He then aimed one near its paw. The monster roared in pain as it stumbled right into a mud pit and sunk into it slowly. Relieved, Scar took a moment to gather himself and catch his breath but quickly remembered there was one left. It saw what Scar did and finally spoke, "You will suffer for that."

The creature growled and charged him, latching onto his weapon and tossed it afar. Scar punched it in the face so he could grasp a sword. The creature put his giant paw onto his chest hitting his metal platter. Growling loudly, dripping spit, which turned into acid that went through the metal. "I'm going to rip off your face!" The beast raised his head high bearing his huge sharp teeth.

Scar hit him in the face few times, then was able to grab his weapon and pierced the creature through his neck upright. The beast shook his head as blood poured out. Scar pushed the animal off him and stood to his feet, sweating and exhausted. He made a smart comment aloud but then heard a loud roar echo. He froze and turned around and saw yet another creature the same that had just perished.

"How many of them are you?" said Scar as he shook his head.

"We are legion!" he stated.

The monster sniffed the air and smelled death. He looked at his fellow comrades, then toward Scar, standing on his hind legs now as his throat began to gurgle aiming for Scar. He reached down and pulled a giant knife from his side leg pocket. Quickly aiming it at his throat, he made a direct hit. The creature bore a look of astonishment in his eyes, then slowly began to burst from the inside near his throat as it then began to expand. Pieces of him flew everywhere, limbs and the head.

Now making his way out from the death trap, he made his way through the jungle stumbling upon a massive village that was made out of hard mud and rock with ancient holographics on them. *Clunk!* Someone hit Scar across the head and began to drag him. Scar awoke tied up with many people watching him, bearing weird-looking tattoos and war paint.

Then finally, the chief approached Scar and asked, "Who are you? How did you find us?"

"Where are my weapons?" A guard hit Scar in the mouth. Scar spat out blood. The chief sternly looked at him. Scar scowled at the man who hit him. "I stumbled upon here accidently after fighting off these creatures." The people began to whisper among themselves.

"Those foul beasts that we call Kadaki fire spitters?" asked the chief. Scar nodded his head.

"Yeah, sure. I took three out." The chief smiled. "This Dr. Montorious supposedly creates these things. I fought a giant crab just before them, and I'm trying to find this man and stop him, but I was told he has an Army and wishes to use it to take over the world." The chief gave a hand gesture. One of the guards untied Scar's hands.

Then he studied Scar. "We know of whom, which you speak. He brought his minions here many fortnights. We need strong warriors like yourself to help. But you alone beat Montorious?" He laughed. "Impossible." The man then spoke in a different language. Shortly after, a man and few others went into the jungle.

"They are going to tell the other tribes we will be taking the fight to him soon."

"I need to find more people in this new world I know nothing of to help, then we will take the fight to him." The man nodded.

"I have ten sons. They all were gifted with the power of extraordinary powers—able to use fire, water, earth, and wind." Scar's eyes widened. "If yet but one of my boys is with this mad titan then." His eyes grew weary.

"Will surely won't have that problem," said Scar smiling. The two shook hands and he then left the village to seek help, not knowing that he'd soon face things far worse than today. Things that'd make your soul cringe. He had to make haste before death came to countless.

CHAPTER 2

The Terrible Fate that Lies Ahead

Scar made his way to the end of the jungle, gazing at the horizon. Pulling out his device, he pressed a button, and a hologram of numerous things appeared. "Ah, this will do." A huge plane appeared. He opened the door, then slammed it. Starting the engine now, and the plane was off soaring over the open sea. Leaving the jungle off to explore this new world. The plane had been in the air for hours now, Scar decided to take a nap. He used autopilot. Scar walked to the end of the plane and lay down. "Wake up, you scum!" Scar awoke surrounded by numerous creatures being different shapes and sizes. He looked up at a man standing in front of him covered in tattoos similar to the people in the jungle. The man grinned at Scar and snapped his finger, and a ball of fire appeared in his hand. "So you must be the one everyone's talking about?" Scar ignored him. The man created an ice crystal in his other hand and threw it at Scar's cheek. He brushed his face against his shoulder.

"Where am I?"

"Isn't it obvious, boy? You've been captured by Montorious."

He looked around and saw his plane had been taken apart. He felt his forehead that had a deep cut on it. Creatures around them laughed. All the sudden a horn was blown, and they all knelt, except for the man with the tattoos. Scar, all of a sudden, was looking down a narrow corridor that seemed to never end, but the figure was still approaching them. The man grew restless and formed an ice spear, piercing him deep in his side. Blood poured out. The man looked into his eyes. "Good night, scum."

Scar gasped for air as he saw he'd fallen out of bed. "It was all a dream," he said to himself, looking now up at the window. It was nearly dark now. Scar got up and went to the fridge as he opened the door. He guzzled down a beverage. A loud boom was heard, which shook the plane. He dropped his can. "What was that? This turbulence is getting bad," said Scar. Now walking to the nose of the plane, taking hold of the controls, soaring higher now over the clouds, almost touching the moon, it seemed, as the stars glistened, and the sky began to turn gray.

Cumulonimbus clouds slowly appeared as it began to rain. There it was again, a loud crackle this time. The plane shook as it seemed to have took weight of something. He unbuckled his seat belt as he pressed autopilot once more. Then made his way to the end of the plane, looking out the window into the peaceful scenery of light rain falling. "Don't see anything," Scar said aloud. Soon as the words were still coming out, he saw but only the giant paw and claws of something walking across the window. It was covered in fur. Its tail almost nearly shattered the window.

It seemed to have three long clubs at the end of its tail. He squinted closer to observe that to be. It had three tongues that were actually snakes looking through the window. Scar ducked down. "Too close," he said. The unknown creature pressed its weight yet again onto the plane. He slowly lifted his head to look out the window. Before his eyes was a horrifying mutated monster that had huge wings with spiked tips at the end, a hard turtle shell, and a grotesque face that had spike tips on both sides of its cheeks. Scar stayed low and crept slowly. Carefully reaching the front of the plane, he began pressing a few buttons. Just as he was about to press the last one to activate weapons, he froze, raising his head up slowly. There at the nose of the plane, pressed against the window, staring him down like a hawk, was the creature. Breathing out smoke from its nostrils, Scar slowly moved his hand toward the button. The beast blinked and stared him down. Then let out an unbearable screech noise. Falling to his knees, holding his ears. Suddenly, two more beasts Scar heard approaching in the distance. "Rip this plane apart!" one of the foul beast yelled. A speaker in the plane then came on. "Defense now initiated." Scar ran to the back of the plane as he put his device into his pocket. The plane electrocuted the monsters off, but one became bold and came back swift. The monster then roared again as he withstood the electrical pain long enough to destroy one of the wings of the plane. Its paw had gotten stuck at the last minute into the turbo, shredding him to pieces, splattering him all over the window. The loudspeaker came on again. "Mayday! Mayday!" Loud buzzing and alarms went off as the plane initiated life reservers that fell down from the top barrier. It continued to blare loud noises, as the plane headed straight for the water below. He quickly rushed through things and put upon a parachute. Knowing he couldn't be anywhere near the plane, for once it hit the water, the electrical shielding would fry him! He then opened the door as high winds whirled, grasping the inside handle to the door tight to prevent from being thrown back further as he turned to look at the nose of the plane to see one of the beasts was breaking through the glass with just his face. He jumped out just in time as the plane crashed into the sea. The beast was smacked down into the water. Scar looked back at the plane as it weighed down the monster, drowning it deep into the seabed. He steered the parachute lowering more to the water. He splashed into the water sinking deep, struggling to remove the parachute. Managing to do so and swimming up back to the surface, he wiped his face, coughing. Now worried where he was, or if there was any land nearby. Scar's eyes raced over the open ocean back and forth. As he then saw a small oasis island straight ahead, he began swimming for it. It seemed so far, but as he drew closer to the small oasis island, he gazed upon a small house and spotted little bridges that were formed high into the trees that led into the small forest.

Stopping to catch his breath, he began to feel his side cramp up. "This is just great! I've been through some bizarre things already. What's next?" he said aloud. Shortly interrupted by a loud noise as he turned to see one of the flying creatures he'd encountered flying fast toward him. He looked in awe for a moment as he began swimming for his life. But the monster was spry and soared low over Scar as he scratched deep into his back. He yelled as blood ran down his back, so he dived deep under the water to escape this persistent creature.

Nearly at the shore, he swam back up, hoping his predator wouldn't be waiting. He gasped for air and breathed heavily. Then up at the sky. "It disappeared just like that." Scar swam a few more feet as he could till he was able to stand in the water, making his way to the mysterious house, dragging his feet in the sand, like some drunkard. Struggling to make it any further to the house, he collapsed, slowly closing his eyes. Shortly after, he could feel someone dragging his body. Slowly reopening his eyes to see a figure that appeared human. He then closed his eyes again. Not knowing who this person was, whether they were friend or foe, it didn't matter, for he was too weak to do anything. He awoke later. The bright sun beamed in through the window. He heard the waves roaring in, splashing against the beach.

Scar tried leaning out of bed. A sharp pain shot up his back. He touched his back to feel that it'd been bandaged, then slowly got out of bed. He shouted, "Hello!" but no answer, then looked at the end of the bed to see some clothes laid out, apparently, for him. Staring at them for a moment, then looked around as he began to change, slowly putting upon the shirt for his back was still tender. He then yelled out once more, "Hello! Anybody there?" But there was still no response. Walking past many interesting photos of great battles and such other things.

He was just about to head downstairs as he stumbled upon a picture of a beautiful woman and saw her holding her child as well. Finally going below, Scar heard a loud noise, a clanging sound as if someone was hitting something. Scar made his way to the back and went outside. It grew louder now. He walked to the front of the house as he looked across the ocean to see sea animals frolicking in the water. He noticed some stairs that led to a bridge leading across into the forest. Scar made his way up the stairs, halfway across the bridge split into two directions.

He stopped to decide, which route to take. The noise came once more from the left. Proceeding further, the bridge rattled as he finally made his way to the end to see a man building a sword. He looked up to see many other weapons hanging.

Before he could speak, the man spoke in a deep voice, "I see you're recovering well." The man looked up at him having a scruffy beard.

"Oh, yes, thank you. If you hadn't helped, I would have died.

"Well, heck, if I hadn't, you'd probably would have stinked up my island." The man grinned. Scar then slightly smiled. "So what's your name?" asked the man, continuing to build his sword.

"Scar. Yours?" The man put down his tools as he reached out his hand.

"Adam." The two shook and nodded to one another.

"This is a nice place you have here," said Scar. Looking out into the forest, he saw varieties of fruits that hung from trees an bushes. "Place like this I could get used to." He awaited for Adam to reply, but he just kept clanging upon his sword. "So where's your family?"

The clanging of the sword then ceased as Adam threw his weapon onto the floor. Scar slowly took one step back but then looked into the man's eyes and saw much pain.

"I used to live in a divine peaceful place. My family and I were happy. We had many friends and people that lived there as well, but all was lost one fatal day." Adam began to tremble as he closed his eyes for a moment, flashing back, as if he could hear ringing in his ears of yells and screams. Opening his eyes again, he said, "When they came—legions of unforeseen creatures and men that could use these supernatural powers. They destroyed everything!" Scar then quickly remembered that some of the chief's sons were possibly with that evil man, but he said nothing, for he didn't want Adam to think obscene, thinking that he's a spy on their side. Adam began to push things off the table. Scar looked in sadness but said nothing, looking at the ground briefly.

Adam spoke once more, "It happened so quickly. Many people were being captured, but some fought back and perished. Fires broke out immensely everywhere. My wife and child were still inside as I prepared the boat. I ran back, but monsters attacked me before... before—" Adam fell to his knees in despair. "I couldn't save them."

He stood back to his feet. "So I left in the boat. As I looked back to see, they dispatched and spread into groups venturing to other places. A huge man was laughing in the midst of all the chaos. I finally drifted off and stumbled upon this place, now calling it home." Adam then looked out into the forest. Scar then waited to speak.

"I'm sorry for your loss, but there's a way to get revenge." Adam now looked at Scar. "Join the fight against Montorious. As we speak, good forces are at work to bring down this malignant tyrant."

"*No!*" he yelled. "Just leave me. You should be healed up by now, and I'm sure you'll be on your way." Scar looked at the man, then into the forest.

"Sometimes unfortunate events may happen in our lives, and we have no control over them, but we mustn't let it consume us." Scar then began to walk away.

Just as Scar was about to leave, Adam said, "Wait. Do you really think we can win?" Scar smiled.

"Yes."

It nearly dawn now. Scar went to stay the night in the condo Adam had built on the right side of the bridge across the bridge. He made himself comfortable. He was able to reach over and grab colorful fruit from trees. Scar bit into the sweet mouthwatering fruit. He filled himself with fruit, then rested his eyes and listened to the slow roar of the waves coming in from the distance. As Scar awoke the next morning, making his way across the bridge once more and past the house headed for the beach, Adam was out there fishing. He'd already caught many types of sea life. "Morning. Come let us go eat!" said Adam. The two headed to a spot where there was fish already cleaned, squid, and shrimp. They cooked their own food over the fire. As the two sat and ate, they talked about their previous lives before all these interesting events occurred. The two laughed as they drank coconut juice, and this other type of juice that was squeezed from a fruit on the island mixed with wine that Adam had upon his boat along with other things. Days passed as the two got to know each other better and became friends. Scar's wounds healed steadily, while the time being, Adam taught him better sword techniques. When Scar was a boy, his father didn't get the chance to teach him much. He also showed Scar certain fighting techniques when doing hand combat while other days would be with a gun, or something else. Scar also showed Adam how his device worked, which fascinated him very much so.

The two one day sat and ate like they always did. Just another serene day, so they thought.

Scar stood up to witness something approaching in the distance. Adam looked at Scar.

"What is it?" he asked as he stood up startled, then looked in the same direction.

"No, it can't be," said Scar as he cursed, for it was the same creature that had attacked him in the water. "It left to bring reinforcements," Scar muttered to himself. Flying behind the creature were eight more similar. He saw giant crabs beginning to emerge almost to shore as dozens of men and Kadaki fire spitters came in every direction as well surrounding the oasis island. More unusual monsters both unseen by both Adam and Scar were coming. "We must hurry! Prepare for battle!" yelled Scar.

"No!" yelled Adam. Scar then made a livid expression on his face, but Adam then faced him and spoke. "I'll hold them off. You go and continue your quest. Defeat Montorious and find more people that will help fight." Adam then ran inside but quickly returned having two guns on his sides, a sword on his back, and yielding a shield on his arm. The loud roar of boats came closer. "*Go now!*" yelled Adam. Scar gave him a look. "I wish not to do this." Scar then nodded. "Till next time," said Adam as he smirked. The two shook hands. Scar then ran quickly to the far end of the island, pulling out his device to find a boat turning to see his friend was fighting valiantly, shooting off multiple rounds. Creatures and men at once. Limbs of crabs, bodies of men, and Kadaki laid dead, but more came. A huge hologram appeared in front of Scar. He began pacing through quickly. The ground then suddenly began to rumble. He fell to the ground, looking up in the opposite direction to see a man with a black hood on have his hands in the air as the ground split.

His eyes glowed dark green. Scar then quickly rose back up. Finally, he then pressed the picture of what he wanted, and his device made a funny noise, then a loud beep! A bright light occurred, and a huge boat appeared before his eyes in the water. Quickly boarding, he ran to the controls as he pressed a button on his device one more time and a robot appeared that steered the boat for him. Scar walked to the back of the boat to see his new friend, Adam, surrounded by men that could use these supernatural power, some formed ice spears in their hands and fire. Beasts that stood by them growled. He looked upon Adam as he stood trembling, exhausted from fighting as blood dripped from his swords.

While the boat drifted further away, all Scar could hear was Adam shout, "*Well, come on then!*" They all then swarmed him and attacked. As Scar could see no more, for he was out of sight, he put his head down in shame, for he knew Adam was dead, and it was all his fault. But he failed to see one last boat that was far from the battle and saw him leave. The man put his hand into the water as it began to swirl. "*Go!* Follow that boy and kill him. Do not fail me, Nikato." Raising his hand out now, a huge monster shadowed underneath the boat, making a disturbing noise as the boat shook. The man grinned, for he knew the evil he'd unleashed upon Scar, for it would change his fate and the journey ahead.

CHAPTER 3

River of the Dead

D ays passed as Scar drifted further out to sea, hopelessly losing his mind, blaming himself for what happened to Adam. He could still hear the yells he made out as he fought. Scar cursed, "I should've gone back," slamming his hand down on the deck railing, then looked down at the water staring down at his reflection, then at the sky as the sun began to rise and birds flew through the air. Scar walked to the front of the boat. Now seeing he was completely in a different place, once again. He pondered to himself what new people he'd encounter, or monsters. The boat went with ease through debris, passing many oddly sculpted statues. Rain began to fall. Scar got up and walked below to his room, figured getting some sleep would help. He awoke the next morning and made his way up to the deck but could barely see. Fog had engulfed the entire area. The robot manning the ship turned on the lights, for it somewhat helped. He looked further out, and it seemed as if something in the fog was moving, coming toward him. He squinted trying to get a better look, as fog then suddenly blew gingerly into Scar's ear as he heard whispers, "You will fail." Scar's eyes grew wide. The voice came again, "This journey mustn't go on."

Scar then began to see dozens of ghost creatures, evil fallen monsters, some bearing long tails that had spikes running down their backs. Others with four arms, and some that had a huge mouth where their stomach should've been. Many were also human, but others had giant wings with many eyes covering their body. The ship traveled further through the fog, but every few feet, it became thicker. A chill ran down Scar's spine.

"*Go away! Leave me alone!*" Scar yelled loudly. But all he could hear was loud crackling of many voices in the fog.

"You dare speak to us in that tone?" one asked. "We're rulers of the Bonteka Lake, for this is where souls go when they are grieved with guilt."

Scar still couldn't see any of the ghosts now. They mostly shimmered and flew throughout the fog near him, seeing only glimpses of the foul beasts. "Why must I end my journey?" Scar asked but heard nothing. The fog became silent now. "I know what I must do!" he yelled. "For I will defeat *M-o-n-t-o-r-i*—"

While the words were still coming out, dozens of ghouls flew lighting fast toward him out of nowhere, coming in different directions all yelling, speaking at once, "You dare speak his name?"

"You fool!" yelled another.

"You will die before you even lay a finger on him!"

When the ghost yelled, water then exploded out of the lake as if a volcano had erupted. It was so powerful, it shook the whole ship and made Scar fall, rising back to his feet.

"You have no Army. Thousands more join him every day. You have no one, boy. You're alone. Go home."

Suddenly, one of the ghostlike creatures shaped into Adam. He had cuts all over his body, and his head was leaking.

Scar fell to his knees as the fake Adam spoke, "You couldn't even save me a supposable friend. You're weak." The ghost's eyes glowed red. Scar shook and trembled. The ghost laughed, then changed back to his hideous form. Slowly, Scar began to build up with anger inside. He balled up his fists.

"Stop it" he said. But the laughs continued. "Stop it!" yelled Scar again. He then charged the ghost, reaching out his hand and somehow grasped its neck. "I said be quiet!" All the ghosts stopped shimmering and were astonished from what they just witnessed.

"How is this possible? No one can touch us," said a ghost.

"Unless—" said another.

"It cannot be!" one yelled in fear.

"Maybe he can," spoke another.

"*Silence*!" one ghost yelled to another.

All the ghosts then suddenly burst into mist that sprayed down auroa disappearing. Then another. One was left. He just stared at Scar, giving him an evil look as he began to float backward into the fog. But then suddenly appeared spontaneously behind him, speaking in his ear, "You will die, boy." It smirked, then burst into a dark auroa as the rest. Scar just sat down trying to take in all that just happened. Looking up ahead to see finally light, and a huge weight that was lifted from him as if life had come back into him. Seems as if it was taken away just for a moment. Loud growling then suddenly occurred.

Scar felt his stomach. "Gosh, I'm starving," he said to himself. He then looked to the side of the boat to see many fruit trees, similar to such back on Adams small island. But some weren't. Scar's stomach growled yet again. "Stop the ship!" he yelled up to his robot. A loud abrupt stop occurred, and a long ramp came sliding out mechanically connecting to the forest ground. Scar left the ship and began picking tons of varieties of fruit and putting them in baskets but knew he needed more hands, so he reached for his device in his pocket, pressing a button that made more robots appeared. He told them he needed their assistance, so they obeyed and did as so, carrying baskets of fruits and other tasty treats back to the ship.

Scar walked a little farther into the forest to find some meat. Continuing to walk a bit more, as he began to get restless, Scar sighed. "No luck," he said aloud. Just as Scar was about to turn back, up ahead, he saw a group of wild boar passing through. Having already out his bow and arrow in hand ready. Steadying his bow, he shot one, piercing the boar in its stomach. The rest then ran in every direction. Shooting off more arrows repeatedly, two more boars had gone down. Scar walked to one, as he retrieved his arrow, then did the same with the rest, putting them back in his holster. Scar then picked one up, throwing it over his shoulder. He then yelled for his robots to assist.

As the three began their way back, loud stomping throughout the forest suddenly occurred. Swarms of birds flew out of the trees. "We must hurry!" yelled Scar. They all then quickly ran the rest of the way, safely making it back upon the ship. The ship then slowly pressed on. Scar's eyes were sharp, looking into the forest. He began to see many giant figures moving. Some knocked down trees. He squinted but barely could make out what they were though he saw dozens. Suddenly, he heard loud roaring of other engines overhead, flying over. He looked up to see interesting-looking flying vehicles soar over the air, that were too high to spot him. He used a telescope to spot thousands of men inside each vehicle. Flying beasts of all kinds flew behind. There were so many that they covered the entire sky. "So it has begun," he muttered to himself.

His heart dropped as he lowered his head in pity, in doubt. "How can I ever find enough people to defeat this seemingly unstoppable force?" he muttered to himself. Then he thought back on what the ghost had said, wanting to prove him wrong. But just sighed, then looked into the direction he was headed. Scar squinted to see dozens of ships far away, going the same way. He then went below to his kitchen to fix up the food he'd caught. After it was ready, Scar grabbed some fruit and juice, then went back up to the deck and sat down. The sun began to set as the air became cool.

A loud thump then was heard suddenly, as if something was on the look out on top of the ship. Scar got up and walked over to it as he saw nothing, so he casually made his way back to his food but stopped as he gazed upon an unusual-looking bird creature that was eating his food. It had a long scorpion tail with pointy ears and a beak the shape of an owls. "Hey, get away!" Scar yelled at the creature, who looked up. It appeared to have three snake eyes.

Scar was in such awe. He couldn't speak. "I'm starving. Leave me be," said the creature.

"This is my boat, my food! You go!" said Scar demanding, becoming impatient. By now, the rest of his food was unfortunately gone. *Burp!* As the creature fell on his back and stared up at the sky.

"Not bad. Have any *d-e-s-s-e-r—*" Before he could finish his sentence, Scar swatted him with his plate. *Wham!*

"Who are you? And where did you come from?" he demanded answers.

"Ease up, pal," said the bird, shaking his head from being disarrayed for a moment. "I'm just passing through." The bird then tried piercing Scar's hand with his scorpion tail but missed and had got it stuck in the table. Now looking upon Scar who had a dagger to his throat, the bird creature swallowed hard. "Okay. Okay, my name is Floyd, and I've traveled far from leaving"—the bird then looked around, afraid of what he was going to say and who else was listening possibly—"Montorious's lair."

Scar then dropped the dagger and backed up in astonishment. The bird finally got his tail free, flew up, and posted himself along the side rail of the ship.

"How did you? Why did you leave?" asked Scar, now moving closer back to the table. The bird took a moment and cleaned his feathers, which Scar saw that had spike tips up top on both wings.

"He's insane, and I want no part in his evil plans to rule the world, even though he created me and many others." The bird sighed. "Here I am now, trying to find a place to stay, have refuge from him."

"But if what you say is true, wherever you go, he'd find you eventually and kill you," said Scar.

"This is true," replied the bird.

"So join me!" said Scar energetically. "I'm on my own quest to find as many people and other beings that would assist in this rise of an evil that's so prime." The bird was so shocked of his words that he fell on his back, then got himself together and stood back up.

"I'd be a fool to go back and try to stand against him! Have you not heard about his infinite Army? He has unnatural power as well. Bet you didn't know that, did you? I've seen all the horrors," Floyd said fearfully.

Scar was now silent for a moment. "All you speak may be true. But I must do what needs to be done, for evil will always prosper when good men stand back and simply do nothing. Turning a blind eye from what you see is just as bad." Floyd then lowered his head in shame.

"You're right." He lifted his head. "I will assist you in this bold attempt to stop him, help any way possible. Though we may die. His fortress is far from here, near the mountains of Kasanaski. It will take many days to get there."

"Well, good. We'll need an Army anyway," said Scar proudly. Floyd then flew upon his shoulder. Scar's eyes then grew big as he stared at Floyd's feet and saw he had one big claw similar to a raptor in prehistoric time, just a tad smaller. The rest were tiny claws along both feet.

At that moment, the whole ship shook like it had hit something. Or something hit it. "Ouch!" Scar yelled as Floyd was so startled, he dug his big claw right into his shoulder unknowingly. "My apologies, my friend!" Floyd then flew up in the air, then over the water to see if he could spot what had caused the massive shake. Scar then ran to the other side of the ship. "I don't see anything." He looked from left to right. But it was so murky and covered with debris, it was impossible to see. "Gather weapons. Be ready for anything!"

Scar yelled to his robots. They rushed around, preparing. "I don't see anything!" yelled a robot that was on the opposite side of the ship. Just when it was walking away, an enormous creature shot out of the water and chomped the robot in two, leaving only its other half as it fell on the deck sparking off light, then caught on fire. The beast splashed back into the water. Scar had only seen a glimpse of this new monstrosity that bore giant spikes that ran down its back. A loud noise came from the water. Robots charged their laser guns and put them on high voltage. The ship shook yet again. This time not so intense. Robots began firing in the water.

The beast emerged from the water slow, having a long neck as it looked down upon them and growled. It then spotted Scar and knew it'd found its target. The monster had two spikes pointing out of its cheeks and one on its head. Having eyes that were silver, then changed to have a black split in the middle of both. The monster put his giant foot onto the ship as robots slid to the side while some grabbed hold of anything they could find, then began shooting lasers at it. The monster became enraged, fully standing out the water now was his three tails that had long needles at the end. They pierced robots as he pulled them toward him, flinging them over the ship.

One of his long tails went around and pierced Scar's leg deep. He cried out in agony falling to the ground as it dragged him. Scar struggled to pull it out as he drew closer to the monster but couldn't. The creature roared as Scar was at the edge of the ship. He tried lifting him up to his mouth. Slowly, Scar was lifted off the ground. But the beast then yelled in pain. Scar looked to see Floyd was clawing at his eye, then bit his neck. Then tried to fly back to the ship but flew too low, and the monster's last tail that was in Scar he used to swat Floyd hard against the ship's top window. Scar crawled to a spot as he examined his leg. It was covered in blood. "Fire! Shoot at its neck!" yelled Scar. The monster roared angrily and retreated back into the water.

The ship began to pass by many houses that were in the forest and other huge obstacles in the water. A loud noise then occurred as the engine of the ship caught fire. "Off the ship!" yelled Scar. He then saw Floyd, who was unconscious and knew he had no time to get him. His leg was badly wounded and bleeding out. The ramp slammed down as dozens of robots carried supplies and picked up Scar. "Wait! Grab the brid!" he pleaded aloud. A robot then rushed and climbed up just in time and had jumped off the side just as the ship then exploded.

But the danger hadn't ceased. Scar and his robots were immediately surrounded by men with spears, bows, and arrows. Swords were pointed at them. The monster shortly after came back as the ship was sinking, heading to shore. Dozens of spears were thrown, and arrows were shot but not much of an effect. Then came a tall man wearing a dark-green cloak. He stepped in the water. As his eyes turned the color of fire, the water began to bubble. You could hear loud shrieks of pain as the beast fell onto his back and its skin changed colors as the mysterious person then lowered their hands.

He then turned to look at Scar, walking over. "Ah! What have we here? One of Montorious's spies?"

"No!" Scar yelled in defense. "I'm a simple inventor who's heard of this man and on a journey to stop him!"

"Lies!" one of the men yelled.

"Silence!" shouted the unknown man in the cloak as he took off his hood and removed his cloak. Scar's eyes grew big, for the man had tattoos similar to the people in the village back on the island. "Let him up," said the man in a deep voice. He had facial hair and a black scruffy beard with green eyes. And was broad in shape.

Scar quickly told him about the village he'd been to and what he saw and that the similar tattoos were there on the people. The man then looked puzzled as he pondered for a moment.

"I met the chief—"

"His name is Sepada," said the man cutting him off but then nodded to Scar reaching out his hand. "Name's Rolan."

Scar replied as the two shook, then the two began to walk, while Scar limped, still bleeding, as he tried his best. But he then stopped walking.

"Floyd? Where is he?" His eyes raced but couldn't spot the robot that had saved him.

"That bird creature? My people will take care of him. No worries." He then patted Scar on the back but then finally saw his leg. "You don't look so good yourself. Sit," said Rolan as he tore a piece of his cloak and tied it around Scar's leg. Helping Scar now back on his feet, the two began to walk again.

"Thanks," said Scar as he looked around to see many people making weapons, children running around playing, and many creatures carrying supplies. Scar looked in awe as he pressed even further to see dozens of houses and more people. He then thought to himself for a moment as his heart grew happy, for he hoped now possibly he'd found the Army he was looking for, but he didn't take heart to it. Scar knew it'd take more than some fisherman.

CHAPTER 4

The Gathering

Rolan continued to show Scar many things that he'd had never seen. The two reached an empty house made from bamboo and other material. "This is where you'll stay. You're welcome to anything you need." He then smiled and began to walk away. Before Scar could thank him, he had already left. Scar then stepped into the room. As he looked around to see, there was freshly seasoned fish and other meats in a bowl, varieties of fruit beside it in a basket, and a pitcher filled with some type of drink.

He began to smile as he was about to walk closer to the welcoming things on the table when he stopped. His eyes grew big. "Oh no! I forgot about Floyd." He glanced at the far end of the room, and there was Floyd all nestled, sleeping in a pile of soft leaves. Scar observed him as he drew closer toward his friend, relieved his new companion was safe.

He looked down to see that Floyd had many bandages but seemed he was recovering well. A large yawn then came from Floyd as he stretched out his wings, and his eyes began to slowly open. "Welcome back," said Scar in a proud voice as he nodded. Floyd then struggled to take a stand. Scar assisted, helping him up as he perched himself on his arm. The two then made their way to the table where the appealing food was, and they ate. Floyd slowly bent down to take a bite. "So what's the next plan?" asked Floyd, slowly raising his head back up.

Scar looked at him for a moment as one of creature's three eyes was bandaged up. "We talk with the leader here of this place. Try to convince him to help us."

"Well, what are we waiting for?" asked Floyd as he surprisingly regained his strength to fly and headed to the door and flew out. Scar just looked down. All of a sudden, he could hear loud noises in the distance. Ice shards shot up in the air, then exploded.

Scar rushed to see what was going on, while numerous thoughts ran in his mind. Pulling out his device now, he clicked on a button as two guns appeared in the hologram. He grabbed them. Now almost to his destination, he could make out two figures that were fighting. Scar began to raise his two guns, slowly stepping closer to them. Finally, there he looked around as people were shouting and clapping as if a show was being put on. Scar made a puzzled look upon his face, then looked more closely at one of the persons to see that one was Rolan and the other he didn't know.

Scar found a place and took a seat. While Rolan and the other unknown man walked to their positions, each nodded to one another. Then Rolan's eyes became instantly a different color, glowing green. He then balled up his fists, and the ground a few feet from him began to shake. He yelled and thick roots sprouted from the ground splitting it open, swiftly making their way to the man. He stood still to take them head on. More roots then sprouted right in front of him, grasping him tight.

"He's done for now," whispered a man in the crowd.

"No, look!" yelled another.

The man's eyes then turned red orange as he burned the roots off and smiled. Putting up both his hands, as intense fire came out twelve feet heading toward where Rolan stood. He then raised both his hands up as enormous twisters of water shot out both. Rolan then jumped into the air forming ice spears rapidly, then throwing them at the man, as he then shockingly reversed them back to Rolan by forming high winds spontaneously.

But Rolan was still strong. He quickly pulled out his sword and began slicing the ice spears in tiny pieces, then coming back down to the ground on his feet. The unknown man then charged Rolan. The crowd cheered. As he pulled out two swords that ignited and became on fire, the two clanged against each other. It was epic. Rolan then raised his hand that was free, and out came wind that pushed him backward, making him hit a tree. Rolan then formed three ice daggers and aimed for the man. Two had caught his shirt near his shoulder and the last just above his head. Nearly cutting a few pieces of hair. The man simply melted them off and raised to his feet. The crowd was now silent.

The two men said nothing as they stared each other down. Finally, the man walked toward Rolan as Rolan then formed an ice spear, just in case. But the man reached for Rolan's hand. "The winner!" he shouted. Crowd then cheered loudly. They soon after dispersed going back to their usual activities and duties. Scar knew now was his chance. He rushed over to talk with Rolan. Pushing through people to get by, Rolan and the man glanced at him as he approached. "Ah, Scar! Meet Kanos." Scar then stared at the man as he casually nodded.

"Rolan, we must talk," said Scar abruptly. Rolan's face then became stern.

"What is it?" The man he'd spawned with crossed his shoulders, interested as well.

"I came here, for your help," said Scar firmly. "An evil force, as you may already know, is making its move. I need your help."

"No," said Rolan strongly. "We're preparing to protect only our home if necessary." Scar's face then became weary.

"Rolan, you must take reason. He's coming."

"That is enough!" The entire ground shook. "Do not speak of such foolishness. We brought you here to save you. If you do not like our hospitality, you and your friend can go."

"Brother, maybe he's right. We should listen if Mon——" Rolan stopped him before he could speak his name and just patted him on the shoulder as he took a deep breath. Then turned to face Scar.

"If you can convince the people of the sky to join you, then we will help you."

"Sky?" Scar looked blank in the face.

"A group of mystical people with powers. They have outstanding unnatural speed and psychokinesis capabilities," said Rolan. Their pets look like wolves in a way almost, but they are huge in body mass with red-and-white fur, but their hair can stand up and shoot out deadly quils, and the tails are most dangerous, I think, since it comes out as a whip and sparks yellow-and-white light. If it hits you, then you know."

Scar grinned. Floyd was close by on a tree limb. He heard the whole conversation, soaring down upon Scar's shoulder.

"What're we waiting for?" said Floyd.

"They're called the Hemanda. Kings of the sky, they say," stated Rolan.

"I'll do it," said Scar in an assuring voice. "Just tell me which way to go," said Scar as he was pulling out his device and pressed a button as the hologram, swiping through the hologram to find a vehicle. Once he did, he tapped it as the device shone, and he aimed for an open spot. Instantly, a black jeep appeared.

Rolan and Kanos were amazed. "What is this magic?" asked Kanos observing, impressed.

"I created this device. Anything you need is right here," said Scar in a proud voice.

"Remarkable!" a man yelled out. He then started to open the door of the jeep as Kanos tapped him.

"I'm coming with. You'll need my strength to face the danger ahead and if the Hemanda choose to fight you." Scar then shrugged his shoulders and grinned.

"Hop in." Kanos did as so on the passenger side. Floyd flew in the back and perched himself on the back seat.

Scar then turned the ignition, and the jeep was off, speeding deep into the forest. "Make a left here," said Kanos. Scar then swerved at the last moment to the left. "The Hemanda are said to live high in the trees near the Ontombe Waterfall. It'll take us a day to get there."

"Then we better hurry. Every minute wasted is more time for Montorious to grow stronger." Kanos agreed with Scar and nodded. He drove the jeep for many hours, passing by varieties of interesting-looking trees and vines, or they seemed to be anyway. Some trees had giant holes in them, even looked like they moved. Creatures that were harmless jumped through the trees, and other crawlers scattered across the ground. Floyd and Scar were amazed, for it was truly a divine sight.

The vehicle then suddenly came to an abrupt stop. "What is—" And before Kanos could finish his sentence, he slowly raised himself out the seat in awe.

"What's all the racket?" yelled Floyd in anger. "I'm trying to sleep." Flapping his wings as he flew up to the front, he now saw what the two gazed upon, for it was a horrendous sight. For as far as the eye could see were dozens of huge tents and fires, while thousands of men and monsters clanged weapons. Words couldn't begin to fathom what the three saw that day. It was breathtaking. Scar became enraged inside instead being shocked anymore.

"We should set up camp now," said Kanos looking now up at the sky, for it was almost nearly dark. The three then traveled a bit more to make some distance between them and the camp. Scar then opened the door of the jeep, then pulled out his device, he pressed a few buttons, and a loud noise occurred then a bright light. Before their eyes was a huge tent. The three went inside a huge room, up ahead were spiral stairs that went to two separate beds, and to the left was a couch and further back another room also a bathroom. "Very nice," said Kanos. He then conjured up currents of wind to lift him up to the bedstead using the stairs.

Scar and Floyd then went their separate ways as well and went to sleep. The next morning came swift as the three awoke, ate something, then were off back in the jeep heading to see the mysterious Hemanda.

"Look, I can see it!" yelled Kanos in excitement. The waterfall was barely in sight but could see specs of it.

"We're almost there," said Scar happily. *Crack*! a huge tree fell on the path. Nearly almost hitting the giant lumber, Scar safely stopped the vehicle.

"Well, that's just great!" Floyd yelled. "Now, we'll get there in two days."

Scar pulled out his device and pressed a button and began swiping through numerous things, finally found it. He then stepped out the vehicle and tapped what he wanted.

Instantly, a machine appeared that had many giant circle-shaped razors like a saw. Also a giant metal clamp that looked like a hand to move the huge tree.

"This will take awhile, not too long though. Meantime, let's go look for some food," said Scar.

"I'll search ahead," replied Floyd.

He then flew high in the air, leading far away from his friends. Scar and Kanos began to walk through the woods, hopping over quicksand spots. "*Ah!*" cried out Floyd, who was just up ahead. Scar drew his sword as Kanos's eyes turned clear white, pulling out his two swords that this time shimmered. Running quickly to where they heard their companion shouted. They stopped and looked in awe for standing beside their friend was a huge creature that had wounded Floyd as he laid near a tree behind the beast, as it stared at Floyd with its back turned.

"That'll teach you to betray Montorious!" yelled the beast.

"Hey, buddy!" yelled Scar. "Leave him alone."

Now being able to see his entire body that was covered in white fur with blue zigzags that looked similar to lighting bolts. He had three fingers on both hands that were pointy and giant spikes that ran down his back as he had a long tail with a giant ball at the end, which was covered in spikes. His feet were like his hands—three toes with sharp points. "You want 'em? Come and get him!" The monster then pulled out two swords that bore an insignia on them of some sort. The woods then began to rustle as something was coming. Three more like the previous beast came stomping out. They stood by the first creature they met as he grinned.

Scar charged the four giant creatures, while Kanos stayed behind. His eyes began to glow green. He, too, then charged. Two beasts went for him as he then uprooted giant roots that shot out of the ground and twisted around one of the creatures' body, wrapping around its neck and snapping it. Scar clanged swords with the monster as he fell to one knee. The monster then put all his weight down as he yelled, "*Die! Now!*" The second quickly came roaring, stopping, baring his teeth, dripping slobber. Luckily, Scar had a dagger on his side leg that he then stabbed into the beast's foot he was struggling to have the upper hand with. He cried out in pain lividly as it then swung around its huge ball-spiked tail down on his face, but Scar dived out the way safely. Then jumped in the air onto its back and pierced his sword deep into his back. The creature fell instantly, for it was dead.

Kanos formed two enormous water twisters. He yelled for Scar to bring the other beast to him. While one of the twisters just sucked up the last creature he had fought. Kanos then froze the monster inside, then shattered it, for the beast was no more only in a million tiny pieces. Scar ran fast he could, bringing the last monster to him. But once the beast's eyes saw the twister whirling, he turned and tried to run in the opposite direction, but it sucked him up. Kanos didn't freeze the twister this time. He raised both hands to the twister and made it explode as the creature came tumbling down, coughing out water.

Scar then put his sword to his throat. "So you think you're so smart. We found Montorious's Army!" Kanos yelled.

"Ha, ha, ha! You incompetent fool! That camp you saw was merely a fraction of his true legion! We're just passing through." The beast then grinned.

"To where!?" Scar asked, but the monster was being difficult.

"I'll tell you nothing!" it shouted. Kanos then sliced off the spike ball.

"*Ah!*" he yelled cursing. "To…to Kasanaski Mountain!" he then shouted.

Scar and Kanos then turned and began to walk away but soon after heard loud crackling. Scar then turned around first and walked up to the beast. *Slice!* He took off the creature's head. "He talked too much," said Scar grinning, looking at Kanos.

Then they both quickly ran over to their friend Floyd, almost forgetting about him. Luckily, he was all right, just unconscious. Scar gingerly picked him up as the three made there way back to the jeep as he set him down softly on the back seat. Seeing also that the machine had done its work well. Pulling out his device and aimed it toward the machine as it shone retrieving it. The path was clean as they pressed on. Now dark, the battle had lasted longer than anticipated. Kanos had fallen asleep as Scar looked over, wanting to as well for the epic battle was strenuous. He drove for a few hours, finally to hear the roar of the Ontombe Waterfall. The vehicle came to a stop. Scar decided to rest his eyes for a moment. Before doing so, he gazed upon the clear water and the reflection of the moon that touched gently against it, making the water glisten.

Scar then turned his neck to see how Floyd was doing but suddenly saw something moving in the bushes, then two big red eyes staring back at him just ten feet away. Slowly moving his hand, not breaking eye contact, he tapped Kanos. "Huh! What?" he yelled aloud, confused. A loud howl erupted from the unknown beast as dozens more red eyes blinked out in the darkness, and their tails seemed to spark yellow-white light that radiated. Scar swallowed hard, for he didn't want to meet these fearless creatures but had a feeling he unfortunately would.

"Start the car up," Kanos whispered. The jeep made a unusual noise.

"It won't start," said Scar trying not to panic.

Growling everywhere then commenced. As what appeared to be what almost looked like wolves stepped out of hiding, coming closer to the jeep. Kanos then cursed, "I'll hold them off." Hopping out the vehicle, his eyes glowed orange as he put out one hand and fierce fire came out, rapidly making a line of fire to keep the beasts at bay.

The creatures howled passing back and forth, baring their sharp teeth. "Got it!" yelled Scar. Kanos then rushed back to the jeep as he dived in. Scar then sped off into the distance, but the beasts followed after swiftly. They tried to cut them off as one grew bold and stepped out in front of the jeep. "Just hit it! Don't stop!" shouted Kanos. But the creature then stuck out its hairs like needles, and they shot out an hit all over the jeep. "Duck!" shouted Scar. *Tss!* A tire was hit. Scar tried to control the vehicle, but it toppled over. Kanos then grabbed Floyd to shield him. The three were slightly disarrayed from the crash as they began to hear loud rumbling as the jeep was slowly being lifted off them. Scar could barely see, but he saw many figures surrounding them with bright light that shone from their eyes as the vicious beasts that had attacked them walked back an forth between the mysterious persons. And at that moment, just when Scar began to shut his eyes from all the tiresome events, he knew that he had found the people.

CHAPTER 5

Trials and Tribulations

S car awoke the next day in a strange room that had bamboo-made floor and vines that covered the walls. It also appeared as if the walls were breathing. Mana floated in the air. Scar then rose out of the bed. He looked around the room. "Kanos! Floyd!" he shouted. But heard nothing. Scar then got out the bed, making his way to the door but was greeted instantly by one of the creatures he saw last night. It was fortunately smaller than the previous ones. Baring its teeth growling, Scar took a step back, but the beast then began to wag its tail, then hoped around wanting to play with Scar.

But a broad man then stepped in and spoke in a different language. This made the creature's tail go down. The man then turned to face Scar.

"Are you the leader of this pathetic excuse for a team?" he asked in a deep voice.

"I wouldn't call us all that," said Scar as he made an insulted expression. "But, yes. Yes, I am."

"Then what makes you think you were brave enough to find us? We are the great Hemanda! Kings of the air." Scar just looked down as he observed what the man was wearing, which was all black with two swords that were on his back. "Speak!" he yelled growing impatient.

He somehow lifted him up off the ground using his hand as he balled up his other hand into a fist and swung in midair as wind spontaneously emerged that formed the shape of a fist and hit Scar in his stomach. Finally, he let Scar go as he fell to his knees, breathing heavily as he held his stomach, then looked up at the man in shock of what he'd just done.

"We!" said Scar trying to catch his breath. "We came to ask for your help" stated Scar in a tiring voice. The man's eyes grew interested. "A dark fate has come upon this world by a new form of evil that I did not think was possible. A man named Montorious is planning to take over the world with his relentless Army of monsters and whoever else wants to join," said Scar. The man then huffed.

"I have no reason to care. We, or myself don't know of whom you speak of he is surely no threat toward us."

"But you must have seen his forces! They're everywhere in these woods!" Scar yelled.

The man then formed a dark-purple energy ball and threw it at Scar's chest. This hurt him immensely. The man then used his supernatural speed and was directly in front of Scar's face as he quivered holding his body.

"Do not speak to me in that tone. I've faced many kind of wars before. You're kind is foolish, always starting wars against one another." Scar saw great pain in his eyes. "All evil does is come again," said the man as he briefly looked down, then back at Scar. "We've seen those creatures you talked about and took care of them." He began to grin. Scar now looked shocked only for a moment. "But you must know there's more! Countless," he said in despair. "Once they finish where they started, they'll engulf everywhere, even where you and your people stay soon enough. You can't hide up here forever." The man then grabbed Scar and put him against the wall as he took off his hood that was covered in battle wounds. His sleeve partly showed his arm that had cuts and wounds as well.

"We do not hide. Don't be so quick to underestimate us," he said as his eyes glowed a bright light. He then let go of him as he turned and walked away as he stopped and began to form another energy ball in his hand as he looked at Scar but then stopped, putting down his hand. "Our power is great, and we will protect what is only ours and kill all who disrupt our peace. You and your friends are free to go." The man then walked to the door. As he left, the little creature then followed. Scar quickly rose to his feet to catch up.

"Wait! You must—"

And before he could say anything else, someone lifted him up and threw him across the bridge that was in the air using their psychic powers. He fell hard into a circular arena that was built high in the air. "He said leave." As the man that had thrown Scar came walking along the bridge now just ten feet away in front of him. "But I don't think you hear too well," he said, giving Scar a mean look.

More people like him gathered in on the fun. Scar struggled to his feet. "*Scar!*" Yelled Kanos from afar in a house. He picked up currents of wind and made his way to him helping him up as they then went back to back. He pulled out his two swords that became on fire. "You insolent fools! We came here to ask for your help! Stop this madness!" Kanos yelled.

"They don't care, my friend. I've already tried," said Scar reaching into is pocket to grab his device and pressed a button to retrieve out his armor, sword, and helmet.

"Ha! Ha!" laughed the head guy. "You think your creativity stands a chance against us? Take him!" he yelled. Men surrounding the two charged them as they rapidly formed and threw energy balls from their hands. Scar and Kanos dived out the way and fought tremendously. Swords clanged against one another as Kanos then put his swords back on his side and began to freeze the three foes that were attacking him. Then ran to assist his friend, pulling back out his two swords, but the man that had led the assault crossed his path. They were equally matched using a sword and struggled to over power the other. Finally, the two broke apart as the man threw down his sword and formed a massive dark and purplish energy ball yelling. Kanos threw down his weapons and formed a giant ice crystal ball and yelled. The two were about to throw each of their huge power-surging formed weapons. "*That is enough!*" The two were so shocked by the deep voice, they both powered down, then looked up to see that it was the man that Scar had tried to reason with. "Tambada!" yelled the man from up top glaring down at him. He then walked down to where Kanos was. Scar walked to his friend and the man. The man then stared at the brutally beaten men that were trapped in the ice, then stared at Kanos giving him a look. Kanos then understood, raising his hand toward the frozen men. One by one unfreezing them. They coughed and fell to the ground. "Come with me," said the man in charge that stopped the fighting. Tambada gave the two an evil look as they walked away following the man.

"Where are we going?" asked Scar.

"And where's Floyd?" said Kanos.

"Patience, young travelers" said the man. When he spoke those words, straight ahead was Floyd playing with the smaller woodland creatures and some children. "Looks like your friend made some new friends." He turned to look at them and smiled. Then turned to look in another direction, to his people that were building something and training of some sort. "We will help you in this desperate time," he said in an assuring voice. "I observed you two's fighting skills and power to see if you knew something worthy enough for the Hemanda to follow into battle." He then turned to face the two. "Name's Nabeth." Scar and Kanos then stated theirs and shook his hand.

"So this was all a test?" said Kanos as he laughed partly.

"Yes, I knew that Tambada would act out the way he did. I was just waiting for the right time to intervene," said Nabeth as he grinned.

Floyd then flew over to where the three stood, happy to see his companions were okay. As the beast that Scar had encountered in the room ran up to him licking his hand, Scar then patted him on the head. "They're called Bosari, and they've been our allies for decades. It is said our ancestors fought great wars with these majestic beasts side by side and so we will yet again. You, my friend, may have him." Nabeth now looking at Scar.

"You must accept. If not is to bring dishonor," whispered Kanos.

41

"Yes, it is," said Nabeth smiling at Kanos. His eyes then grew big and embarrassed.

"I accept. Thank you. I'll name him Scout."

Nabeth then nodded. Kanos then told Nabeth that his brother would join them, if they'd convince them. But had no proof when he went back.

"I see," said Nabeth as he reached into his pocket and handed Kanos a circular wooden tablet. "I apologize my pets destroyed your vehicle," said Nabeth as he looked to Scar.

"No worries," he replied.

And the four made there way back down to the ground as Scar pulled out his device and swiped through his hologram, tapping a picture of the device, then shone as another jeep instantly appeared, but this one was red. Nabeth laughed. "You're full of surprises, Scar." Scar then opened the door of the jeep. Scout hopped in the back, and Floyd flew onto the back seat. Kanos then got in on the other side. Scar then turned to face Nabeth. "Do not worry, Scar, we will assist you, for I have thousands of loyal men. We will all fight." Nabeth looked deep into Scar's eyes seriously. "Good will need you. The battle will take place at Kasanaski Mountain." He then started up the ignition. They drove a peaceful drive back to Kanos's village.

Few days had passed finally reaching it. Kanos quickly went to find his brother, Rolan, and handed him the wooden tablet that had a pacific symbol on it that bore the mark for the Hemanda. Rolan's eyes grew big as he then stared at his brother and took a deep breath then exhaled. "My people!" Rolan yelled out. "The people of the lost village live! And so I've made my decision we will help Scar fight Montorious!" People then whispered among themselves. "For we must. Together, we are strong and will defeat this evil!" The crowd then cheered. Monsters and humans alike then began putting weapons in giant objects to be pulled by something as others continued to make more weapons.

Scar then pulled out his device and walked into the water. Kanos quickly followed. Scar then turned around. "I'm coming with you. It seems once again you may need my help, and I'd also like to see the world," said Kanos grinning.

"Well, we better get moving then," said Scar as he slightly smiled, then looked at his device and swiped through it as he stopped and found what he was searching for. He this time reached his hand inside the hologram and threw what was in his hand in the water. It expanded quickly, floating before him was a huge ship. Scar then pressed another button, and a ramp came down to him from the ship. Scout was the first to board the ship, then Floyd, who flew up. And the previous robots before boarded, also carrying supplies. Scar pressed a button that deployed more robots. While Kanos took his time saying goodbye to his brother briefly as the two hugged.

"You watch your back, little brother," said Rolan.

"Don't worry about me, bro," said Kanos as he turned and began walking up the ramp. Robots passed him on the way. Kanos turned his head and yelled out, "It was me who won that duel!" He smiled as he walked the rest way up and leaned on the side of the railing looking at his brother.

Rolan then sighed as he shook his head. "You know, I don't remember it happening that way! I was easy on you, little brother, and you still lost," said Rolan snickering.

Kanos then made a look upon his face of awe, then smirked. Scar then nodded to Rolan as the ramp retracted itself back into the ship. The ship was then off, slowly easing into the sunset, journeying far from Kanos's village. Passing giant hills and canyons, Scar looked over the edge to see dozens of tiny creatures swimming alongside. They had long tails and scaley skin. One then turned over onto its back as its eyes split and became another color staring up back at him for a moment, then swam away. Kanos then approached Scar, looking down at the water also.

"Fascinating creatures, aren't they?" said Kanos.

"Indeed they are, but I wonder what new things will meet along the way." Scar gave his friend a more serious look.

"So how's my father?" asked Kanos, while he stared out to sea.

"Great," Scar replied. "But he does worry that some of you may have joined." Scar paused as he just stared at Kanos.

"Zepa," said Kanos as he looked down. "He, without a doubt, would be with Montorious," said Kanos, slowly raising his head back up, his face expression weary. Scar swallowed hard as his heart grew cold, and a shiver ran down his back, for he had remembered something.

"When I had my plane, and I had left your village," said Scar as Kanos looked at him wanting to hear more, "I went to rest. Then I went into some weird dream state." Kanos's eyes then grew big seeming intrigued. Scar continued to speak. "I was surrounded by monsters and men. One man stood in front of me as he used his supernatural power and later killed me. The weird thing about it, it actually all felt real."

Kanos shook his head and muttered "Zepa" in shame. Scar nodded. "He is the most powerful out of all ten of us, and so when the time comes, I will be the one to kill him, for he's lost his way and will not reason. His powers have consumed him, drove him evil."

Scar didn't say a word, but he wanted to tell his friend of the other person in his dream that was approaching him, but he thought to himself that was enough for today. The sky grew dark, and dozens of stars began to shine and light up the sky.

"You never know, there could be hope." Scar smiled trying to cheer up his friend. While Kanos tried to feel some type of relief or confidence, he then nodded to Scar.

"Well, we might as well get some rest. Who knows what awaits us tomorrow," said Kanos.

"Agreed," replied Scar.

The two went their separate ways and slept. Floyd and Scout were already resting in a nearby corner on the top deck of the ship. The next morning drew near. While the ship began passing small cottages, more were in the distance. Scar awoke and made his way to the top deck to greet his companions to see them all eating and relaxing. "Come join," said Kanos, waving his hand in the air. "If Floyd saved me anything." Scar gave Floyd a look as he walked over and sat down, leaning in to grab a piece of meat. Slash! Floyd's scorpion tail pierced the piece of meat that Scar had been reaching for. He gave Floyd a scowl look.

"Oh, stop it, there's plenty of everything." Floyd stuffed his face eating bits of meat off his tail. Scar shook his head.

"Yet you still insist on taking my food!"

"Gotta let that go," said Floyd smirking. A loud howl then erupted.

"Sorry, looks like they forgot about you," said Scar, ripping of a giant piece of meat and throwing it.

Scout hopped into the air and ran off with it, as he attacked it eating happily wagging his tail that sparked off light. The ship began to pass many small fishing boats as people waved while they passed. Some old people just stared and didn't break eye contact. "Where are we?" Scar pondered out loud. Scar then looked up as they were going under an overpass. A sign hung that read, "*Welcome to Baltar City.*" And below that it had tiny words that read, "Where magic is power." Scar then got up and walked to the front of the ship, while his friends continued to have all the food down without him. They drew closer to a dock as dozens of people walked about and unloaded things as well. The ship then came to a steady stop as Scar let down the ramp. Floyd flew over to him, and the rest of his companions came over to look in amazement of all the things they gazed upon. Soon after they began walking down the ramp, they were greeted immediately by a townsperson, but something else caught Scar's gaze, for he hadn't seen this type of creature before. It looked mean. But then again, aren't they all?

"Hello! Welcome to Baltar!" said the man energetically.

"What?" shouted Scar as his gaze was distracted.

"I apologize" said the man. He then looked into the direction where Scar was sternly focused on. "My, my, marvelous creatures, aren't they?"

"Yes," said Scar tapping his sword. The man then looked down and tapped his shoulder.

"No need for that, my friend. They're our allies and friends, and I doubt you could even take one on."

As the beast drew closer just passing by, he was tall and big with diamond-shaped eyes covered in golden-brown fur. Scar then looked up at its nostrils as steam puffed out, then stared down at its feet that had spiked tips and hands that were the same. His tail was long but seemed to be made of steel. On his left arm was a symbol of some sort with two dots and a swirl in the middle. He also had a strip of hair but ponytailed.

"They're called Mandare," said the townsmen, pulling his bag that was filled with fish.

"Why is that?" asked Scar, making a confused expression. "I'm sorry. Your name is?" asked Scar.

"Typhus," stated the man reaching out his hand, as did Scar told him his, seeing that his friends had already stated who they were. Typhus smiled, then strapped his basket to his back, and began to walk away.

"Well, wait!" Kanos shouted. "Where can we find the ruler of Baltar?" Typhus then turned slightly around as he laughed.

"All the way up there." He pointed way up on a hill across a bridge was a castle and a giant glowing blue-and-black large orb that glowed in an excluded spot that Scar saw and was intrigued by.

"Why, what's that?" he yelled aloud to Typhus. But the fisherman was already gone.

"Well, we better get moving," said Floyd, flying up ahead.

"It'll take us forever to get there like this," Kanos mumbled aloud.

Scar then saw a sign up a head that read, "Rent a horse and buggy for a day." Scar walked over to the man that was sitting on a bucket with a hole in his hat chewing on some jerky.

"Hello," said Scar.

"What'd you say? I have bad ears, son Can you speak a little louder?" Scar then repeated himself speaking louder. "Why, of course!" said the man happily. The man got up slow as Scar insisted on helping. The elderly man walked to his stable. "Why, choose your pick."

"I'll take two horses," said Scar, pulling out some money from his pocket into the man's hand. He then looked down in his hand at the money.

"Why, what the heck is this? Some kind of scam?" the elderly man cursed. "You young people today don't know how to get through this world with making an honest living."

"Why, no, sir. I'm sorry that's all the type of money I have." The elderly man then rubbed his chin.

"Hmm, well what about that fancy gizmo of yours?" Scar looked down on his side holster.

"Why, this is too valuable."

He then paused as he pulled out his device and asked to see what the money that the man insisted on having looked like. The old man then reached into his pocket and pulled out giant coins that were many colors that bore a man's face upon them. Scar then scanned the money as he then shined the device over his money as it instantly became like his. The man cursed again, "Well, I'll be. That's a mighty fine device you got there." He smiled at Scar. He then paid what he owed the man and then hooked the two horses up to the buggy and went on his way. "Wow, got us a ride," said Kanos approaching, holding food in one hand that was on a stick. Floyd flew over head and landed on the buggy. Scout then hopped in he back of the buggy, as did Kanos, while Scar maned the rails as they were on there way to meet the king.

"Do you ever stop eating?" asked Scar briefly looking back at Kanos and Floyd.

"Sometimes you just gotta get your grub on," said Floyd as he fell onto his back, closing his eyes.

"He's right," said Kanos handing Scar some food. Scar then nodded, then took off bits of meat off the stick.

Journeying further into Baltar City, they passed many interesting restaurants, shows, and many other appealing things. Shows that were being played for crowds, this made the three to want to go see what it was about but knew they had a mission first. *This seemed like the place to want to stay*, Scar thought to himself. Finally reaching the castle where there were two giant gold statues ten feet away from each other of a man that seemed upright. "That must be him," said Kanos. As the buggy went into the courtyard where to the left was that interesting glowing blue-blackish ball of light, which Scar observed for a moment to see that it was surrounded and heavily guarded by Mandare. The buggy then came to a stop as two broad men with swords stopped them.

"What business do you have with the king?" asked one of the soldiers as the other gave Scar and his companions a suspicious look.

"Why, it's an urgent message for the king." The men just stared at them for a moment.

"Okay! But make it quick!" one shouted.

The four got off the buggy and entered a huge room that had a giant fountain and Mandare creatures sculpted around it. Well, as two other beasts Scar hadn't recognized. "No one's here?" said Floyd as he flew around the room. Scout began to bark happily. "What is it, boy?" said Scar as he saw a man approaching them, for it was Typhus.

"What are you doing here?" asked Scar as he smiled shaking Typhus's hand.

"Why, I just wanted to see if you guys made it here all right." Typhus partly smiled walking past to greet rest of them.

"Yes, but no luck in talking to the king," said Kanos looking around to see if he spotted him.

"Why, what'd you need to ask him, if I may ask?" said Typhus.

"Well." Scar sighed a moment. Typhus then gave Scar a puzzled look, taking the basket off his back. "We came to warn him about an evil man who created an army of monsters and plans to take over the world."

"*M-o-n-t-o-r-i-o-u-s!*" said Typhus unfearfully as green-and-orange mist covered his body as he slowly became a totally different person wearing different clothes as his hands didn't look all cut up from fishing anymore. He then stepped up the stairs and sat on the throne.

CHAPTER 6

Power Can Be a Curse!

S car and his fellow companions all looked at Typhus in awe.

"You're the king?" Kanos eyes grew big.

Typhus laughed and said, "Yes, I am."

"But how? How did you look one way and now another?" Scar asked aloud.

"Why, it's just one of my tricks, illusions, you could say, or hidden identities. I tend to disguise myself as a person to go out and observe my city and the people that live in it in a different perspective."

"I see," said Scar, looking around the room. Typhus walked down the stairs.

"Come. I have something to show you."

Scar and his friends followed behind Scout who barked running ahead. Typhus turned to the left making his way to the giant blue-blackish ball of light Scar had been constantly seeing. It was an extaordinary sight, as tiny dots inside the ball moved slowly.

"This is how I'm able to do what I can. My power source, or you could say, magic," said Kanos aloud.

"Yes, magic." Typhus waved his hand for the Mandares and said, "Leave us." Loud stomping of giant feet walking away. Scar's eyes grew wide as he looked up at the sky and saw giant winged creatures.

"My gosh, what are those?"

Typhus said, "Come. I want you to meet a Mandare, and I'll show you."

Scar took one last look at the bright giant ball of light. He and his friends followed Typhus. Typhus signaled one of the flying creatures that had landed on top of the castle to come down. It flew low and fast toward them having a giant wingspan with dagger-shaped points in the middle of both wings. On the bottom of each wing were triangle-shaped points. It also had two long tails that were in the shape of a diamond on the end. Its eyes looked similar to the walking-type creatures. Suddenly, as soon as it was nearly six feet from them, it instantly changed form, and it slammed onto the stone ground. As it arose, Scar, Kanos, and Floyd were all in awe, for it became what Scar had first seen when he came to Baltar. How is this possible? As Scar walked closer to the beast, it roared loudly, and you could almost see it kind of smile. Typhus laughed.

"Mandares are shape-shifters. They can become three different creatures. It's simply just what their race is capable of." Typhus smiled and looked up at the beast.

"And what of the third?" Kanos asked, impressed. Typhus pointed.

"Here they come now." Scar looked. He saw dozens of long-bodied reptilian creatures slithering toward them, each having six arms, their mouths filled with rows of sharp teeth, and a forked tongue. "They tend to stay in one natural form and usually only change form when in battle," said Typhus.

"This is still so fascinating. Never seen anything like it. I never thought I'd be encountering things such as this when I wanted to see the world," said Kanos as he squinted his eyes to get a closer look.

"Come," said Typhus, "a feast shall be prepared. It's not every day I get new visitors to my city. We can also discuss more of why you've come here," giving Scar a more serious look.

"Of course," said Scar, nodding his head, and the two began to walk back into the castle well as his friends and pet, Scout, followed behind.

"Jasper! Telina!" yelled Typhus. Two people came rushing toward him. They both bowed.

"Yes, my king?"

"Please show our guests to their rooms while they wait to eat."

The servants led Scar and Kanos to their rooms. A few hours later, they went back to the main hall, then to the right into another huge room filled with many long and round tables. The room quickly filled with people that lived in the castle and some who didn't. "Scar!" Kanos waved his hand. Scar and Kanos saw Typhus was sitting at a much-bigger table with higher-ranked people and a woman who sat beside him. They walked over.

"Come meet my queen, Aridonna." Kanos and Scar bowed.

"Why, hello! It's nice to meet you." The queen gave them a kind smile.

"Yes! Yes!" said Typhus, who was eager for Scar to meet his friends. The first was Aphemis to be introduced. He was a muscular guy that was drinking a lot. "Meet Scar!" said Typhus smiling happily, but the man just stared at Scar and gave him a side look. "Oh, don't mind him. He's just still mad about loosing that bet!" Aphemis partly laughs as he takes another sip of his wine. Then there was Ramos who was broad with a big belly. Scar shook the greasy man's hand. The man laughed.

"Sorry about that. These cookings got my hands full!" Scar made a gesture as he casually wiped his hand on his pants.

"Ah! Well, come eat, Scar!" Putting up his hand, he pointed to a long row of people. "You can meet the rest soon. Sure, you're starving," said Typhus. Scar nodded and followed the king to his seat beside him. "It seems your friends didn't wait for you." Typhus laughed. He leaned down to see where Scar's friends were and sat. Scar was covering his face with his hand.

"Of course," he said, embarrassed.

He then began to eat as well, for it surely was a feast—endless rows of varieties of fruit, meat, sweets, soups, and salads. If you were standing from afar, everything looked tasty.

"Food's great!" Kanos yelled down to Typhus.

"Thank my servants. They prepared it." Kanos nodded and partly smiled.

"Yes, it is," said Scar agreeing with Kanos as he took a drink of some sort of tasty liquid.

"So now, to talk about business," said Scar, then looked at Typhus as his mood changed and his people who were laughing an eating. "You already know of you know who?" Scar asked.

Typhus sighs. "Yes, because he came to me asking for me to become his ally to join him. He was also very interested in the Mandare creatures."

Scar nearly dropped his glass while he was taking another sip. "Is everything all right?" asked Typhus's wife as she touched his arm.

"Yes, my dear," he said, smiling an trying to reassure her.

But she only slightly smiled, still showing a concerned look upon her face. She then began talking to the person next to her once more. "You've seen him?" asked Scar, paused in shock.

"Yes," said Typhus as he took a drink of his wine.

"What's he look like?" Scar said, looking afraid of the answer.

"*Death.*" Typhus seemed too afraid to describe any more at this time. Scar took a deep breath and said nothing. "After I declined his offer, he later sent his forces to attack, and they were searching for something, it seemed.

"And that was?" asked Scar, Typhus stared at Scar.

"My power source you saw." Scar looked in awe. But why? Typhus's eyes grew weary.

"I'm not sure, but what I do fear is that they will return again, and this time with greater numbers." Typhus looked down for a moment. "Come. Let us walk." Typhus stood up out his chair. Everyone in the room did so as well. As Typhus and Scar walked out, everyone sat back down again. Typhus and Scar went down the hallway onto a huge patio that overlooked the entire city. "Look at all this," said Typhus as he looked down at Scar, then back upon his city. Scar gazed out, looking upon many lights and people roaming the streets, walking and laughing at the giant fountains that flowed clear water and at the Mandares patrolling the sky and streets. "All you see will be desecrated if I help you stop him." Scar looked out once more, and he spoke again.

"But if you do nothing, it will anyway." Typhus turned his head, slightly angry. "You said so yourself. His forces may attack to steal your power source. You must be ready for the war to come, for it's inevitable. So many have joined me, each all bearing unique powers, but it's still so little compared to what Mon——" Scar stopped himself and said, "We need you," giving Typhus a serious look. "How can you just sit back and let evil become so much stronger than you? As it swarms over this earth like a plague, only getting hungrier. He will, no doubt, not leave you and your people unharmed, for Montorious is truly a monster. Join me." Scar reached out his hand. Typhus looked at Scar, then upon his city, sighing as he shook Scar's hand.

"For freedom." Typhus smiled. "Now let us return to the feast." He put his arm over Scar's shoulder and made their way back to the feast area. Everyone stood up once more, then sat back down when Typhus did. The rest of the evening was filled with laughter and peace as Scar yet again felt like this was the place to be where you could call home. As the day began to come to an end, people began to disperse and go home, some just stood around and talked in groups. Scar and his companions headed straight for bed. Floyd on Kanos's shoulder was already falling asleep, snoring extremely loud.

"He can stay with you." Scar gave him a look.

"Great," said Kanos sarcastically, mumbling to himself since he was so exhausted. He opened the door to his room as did Scar. They were just across the hall from each other. Quickly, they both went to bed. The next day came, and Scar was awakened by loud noises of some sort, as if a festival was being put on. Rising out of bed, he looked down at Scout curled up still sleeping. He laughed as he lifted off the covers and made the bed. He then refreshened himself in the bathroom, shortly later, making his way to the door. Scar gave a whistle and said, "Come on, boy." Scout's ears perked up as he rushed to Scar's side. Scar opened the door and went over and knocked on

Kanos's door to see if he and Floyd were awake. He knocked, but there was no answer, so he knocked harder. "Kanos! Hmm, they must be already out exploring Baltar," Scar said to himself. Making his way now down the hall, he turned left almost to the front gate. He stopped to see there was some food and other refreshments upon a table.

"Take as much as you like," said Telina, one of the servants, who was approaching.

"Oh, why, thank you." Scar smiled taking a handful of some type of nuts and grabbing a sandwich that was wrapped up still warm. She slightly bowed.

"I apologize. There isn't much left. Your friends sure had quite an appetite." Telina smiled.

"Why am I not surprised?" Scar shook his head. She laughed. "Do you know where they went?" asked Scar.

"They said they wanted to see the sights, and get some good food." She smiled once more, and for that split second, Scar felt like he was somewhere else. He'd never really taken the time to gaze upon her beauty that he admired so very much. She had long dark hair that was mixed with light brown. She also had bright green eyes.

"Oh, yes. Yes." Scar tried to get out of the trance he was in.

Telina smiled and asked, "Are you okay?" She had a slightly concerned look on her face.

"I'm fine," said Scar giving her a smile. He began to walk away, then slightly turned back around and said, "Thanks."

Telina slightly bowed, and Scar continued to walk away. He made his way out the front gate and over the bridge into the noisy streets of Baltar. He tried to think which way they'd gone. He began to ask around, asking people if they'd seen a scorpion-tailed bird and a man with tattoos with a certain design but no luck. "Come on, Scout!" Scar shouted as he saw him trying to play with a toad at a near by a sewer. He heard loud barking behind him, then heard the loud trotting of paws splashing in mud. Scar passed by many interesting stores and decided to take a peek inside one, hoping he'd come across his friends as well. Opening one of the doors, it rang.

"Hello! Welcome. Come in! Come in! Please." Scar was quickly greeted by a short man wearing baggy clothes and a big hat, but he looked strong and was broad.

"Hello," said Scar nodding. Scar then stated his name.

The man nodded and stated his name "Oscar."

The man began to walk around the store showing him unusual types of food, but he also had impressive varieties of weapons and clothes for sale. There was a white cloak with a hood that had a giant design on the back of it. The same symbol the Mandare had upon his shoulder.

"I'll take it," said Scar, and he pulled it off the rack happily observing it more.

"Why, a fine choice indeed!" said Oscar energetically as he then rushed Scar over to try a sample of some food. But Scar was mistaken. Oscar had handed him a bowl filled with slimy, grotesque eyeballs from some creature. "They're called Garleo eyeballs, and they are just to die for! They come from these giant fish, which are very rare to catch." Scar looked again inside the bowl, then at the man. He tried to keep a calm face, but the repugnant smell that the fish eyes gave off was unbearable for Scar.

"No, really, I'm fine. I'll pass." But then Scar saw something he did want, for the only thing that looked safe to eat was chicken, walking casually over to it.

"Wonderful!" yelled out Oscar, overjoyed, but as Scar drew closer, he saw it began to move in a way. As he squinted his eyes, there were tiny hairs all over it. Scar's eyes grew big as he put a hand over his mouth to stop himself from becoming sick.

"On second thought," said Scar as he pulled himself together, "I just ate. I'll just pay for this and be on my way."

"Why, of course." The man humbly nodded his head and went to the counter, but as Scar made his approach to the register, he saw one of Typhus's men in the far back of the store observing something he held in his hand.

"Sir?" The man tried to get Scar's attention as Scar looked even harder to make out who the man was, for it was Aphemis. "Sir!" the man said once more. "Mr. Scar!"

"Oh, I'm sorry." He handed the man the money, as Scar then looked to see if Aphemis was still there, but he was gone. Ringing of bell. He just left Scar murmured to himself as he quickly grabbed his bag and followed after him.

"Thank you! Come again!" yelled out Oscar as he was already outside his store where Scout had sat waiting patiently for his master. He looked both ways to find, which way he went as he saw a man way ahead to the right, which Scar had a hunch it was him. Scar hurried off in the direction Aphemis had gone as Scout was right behind. They then passed a store filled with many paintings as a rush of people then came out in between them in the direction they were going, as Scar was going as he and Scout got separated. Scar yelled out for Scout as he continued to walk looking back to see if he could spot him. He was suddenly slammed against a wall while a knife was put to his throat.

"Why are you following me?" Aphemis said, staring Scar in his face while smoking a cigar, smelling like liquor, looking angry. "Talk!"

"I just wanted to say, 'Hey.' Never really got the chance to meet you." Scar raised his hands up a little in defense.

"Lies!" He cut Scar's arm slightly. "Tell me why you came here to Baltar. Why'd you talk to our king?"

"That's none of you're concern." Scar gave Aphemis a mean look as well.

"Mind your tone, boy. That's tough talk coming from a man with a knife to your throat." Scar said nothing but looked him straight in the eyes unfearfully. Scout ran up and bore his teeth, ready to attack.

"It's okay, boy." Scar lifted his hand up slowly and made a gesture to calm him down. Aphemis then turned the left corner of his eye as he was somewhat intimidated by Scout.

"I know why you're really here. You and your friends are spies for Montorious." Aphemis said his name low so no one could hear. He then grabbed Scar's body and shook him, making Scar's head hit the wall. "Shut up! Can't fool me! You came here to steal our power source. I've seen the evil bird thing you have before," he whispered in Scar's ear. You may have everybody else fooled but not me. As Aphemis began to lose his balance, he fell backward a moment, for he was a little drunk. Scar now had the opportunity to run as he searched for an exit. His eyes saw a huge crowd cheering and laughing from afar, watching an act of some kind. He noticed in the very back he saw Kanos with Floyd on his shoulder.

"He's changed now," said Scar as he turned to face Aphemis.

"Liar!" Aphemis yelled loud enough to where Floyd heard him over the loud crowd as he turned his head all the way around to see Scar helplessly being held against the wall by a huge man. Floyd flew over.

"Is there a problem here?" Floyd had his scorpion tail ready to pierce the man's neck as he hovered right behind him. By this time, Kanos realized where Floyd went off to as he rushed over and formed two ice balls with sharp quils covering them that didn't seem to be able to prick him.

Aphemis then looked over at Kanos then behind him at Floyd as he said, "*No.*"

He let go of Scar and whispered, "Till next time" and walked off as he lit up another cigar and flicked the other to the ground.

"What was all that about?" asked Floyd.

"Yeah," said Kanos who was also curious as he powered down the ice balls in his hands.

"Nothing. I'll tell you later." He held his arm while blood ran down. "Let's just enjoy the rest of the show." He pointed in the direction that the show Kanos and Floyd were originally at as they all walked over. A person was behind a curtain putting up Mandare puppets. Kids laughed and clapped.

"Must be a new show going on now," said Kanos as he watched uninterested.

"Then let us press on." Scar led the way, and Scout ran alongside him as his friends followed behind.

"Hey, what's that?" Floyd stared into Scar's bag at the cloak he had bought. Pulled it out the bag.

"Whoa, that looks really interesting—the design. Put it on!" yelled Kanos. Scar put his arms through the sleeves as he put the hood over his head.

"Nice," said Floyd as he flew over to observe the back, then the front.

"Where'd you get it?" asked Kanos as the three began to press on once again.

"Oh, from this store on the side of the street close to the castle. It had lots of interesting things inside," said Scar as they all stopped into a store that had jewelry inside. Scar picked up a shiny green jewel. "This would match perfectly with Telina's eyes," he muttered to himself.

"Say what?" Kanos looked confused. Scar quickly put the jewel back down.

"Oh, nothing." Scar tried to play cool.

"No, you were talking about the store you were in. Are you okay?" asked Kanos.

"Yes. Yes, the store." Scar completely ignored his question. "They also had food there but, food!" Floyd flew over to where his friends stood.

"Where?" Scar pointed out the door.

"That direction." Floyd flew out the store fast, and Kanos rushed out the store.

"Then let's go!" Floyd tried to rush Scar, both of them eager to leave.

"You don't understand this food was—" And before Scar could say another word, his companions were already fifteen feet ahead. Scar sighed. "Come on, Scout." Scar waved his hand in the air, then rushed to keep up with his friends. While ahead, they were stopped by a large crowd. A dance was being put on. Applause. People cheering.

"Ah, how long is this gonna take?" yelled Floyd as he flew high in the air to see if there was a way around.

"Just relax, Floyd," said Kanos. "We're going to try the great food that's there."

"I told you guys for the last time. If you give me a chance, the food looks horrible! Some had hairs and muck inside. A bowl of eyeballs as well. It was a nightmare of horrors."

Floyd and Kanos then gave Scar a blank disgusted look as they both said, "*Yeah*, never mind." All Scar could do was cover his face.

"I tried to tell you." He began to laugh. But the dancing suddenly stopped as people began to look up at the sky, not moving a muscle. "What's going on?" Scar asked aloud as he and his friends looked up at the sky in awe. Dozens of giant fireballs flew over the city. *Boom!* The first fireball impacted as debris blew, and stone began to crumble off buildings as it fell on people and as fireballs hit people, making them turn completely into ash. People ran around screaming in every direction trying to avoid the danger.

"Kadaki fire spitters," Scar said aloud to his team.

Floyd cursed, "Even here, they find me." He lowered his head in shame.

"I don't think they're here for you," said Kanos as he dodged a fireball and froze another coming at him, then instantly made it hot as it simply then melted and became mist.

"Agreed," said Scar as he hid under an overpass.

"Come. I must find Typhus!" Waving his hand to his friends. "I'll tell you on the way." Whistles. "Scout, let's go!" The three rushed to make there way to the castle, as along the way, Scar told them what he an Typhus had discussed. Montorious's forces had already breached inside at every angle from giant crabs, Kadaki fire spitters, men, and Crokinians. They all fought dozens of Mandare neck to neck as well as Typhus's soldiers. Scar and his friends rushed passed thousands of people trying to escape the horror. "We're almost there!" yelled Scar as they were running to the bridge. Nearly there, Scout right behind was keeping up until a giant monster blocked their path. As they all were sweating and breathing heavily, they stared in awe. This beast looked even more dangerous than the previous things they'd encountered, for it had four arms all yielding different kinds of swords. Each of his hands had giant pointy claws including his feet, and his face had eight eyeballs running vertical down his face but one big one in the middle. He had two pointy ears shaped as an elf, but the most hideous thing of all was where his mouth was. Dripping off his body on to the ground was saliva and drool, for his mouth was where his stomach appeared not to be!

"Which one of you is ready to die first?" yelled the beast. Scar quickly got his sword out from his remote.

"*Me!*" yelled Kanos as he stepped in front of Scar wielding his two swords.

"Kanos!" yelled Floyd.

"We all can fight together!" yelled Scar.

"No, from what you've told us, you haven't much time left. Get to the power source and protect it at all costs!" yelled Kanos. Scar nods.

"Let's go, Scout." He barked.

"You, too, Floyd," said Kanos. "I'll be okay, pal." Floyd stared at his friend for a sec.

"Okay!" He flew off swift catching up to Scar.

Kanos then cursed at the monster, "Well, let's do this already!"

Then yelling as his two swords suddenly became on fire. He then charged the monster as it then did the same. Kanos then jumped into the air coming back down hard onto the creature, but it was no fool for it covered it's face as his tongue wrapped around his leg an threw him seven feet. As Kanos still had both swords in his hands, this time, the monster charged him while he was still on the ground. Meanwhile, Scar was almost to the power source. As you could hear yelling up ahead, Scar finally made it to the courtyard as Mandare fought air donos, the creature that attacked Scar's plane. He looked up to see flying Mandare that shot diamonds from their tails piercing a flying beast in it's neck as it went tumbling to the ground. Scar then from afar saw Typhus battling another new creature that was enormous as it had a giant M on its right arm. Scar quickly pulled out his remote as he got out the rest of his war gear on, helmet, and all. Then charged to the front gate slicing through monsters, making his way to Typhus as Scout and Floyd followed behind doing what they could. Still fighting his way through the drastic attempt to his friend, he saw Typhus being picked up as he was then thrown against a wall by the creature he was fighting. Four soldiers immediately ran to their king as eight more soldiers charged the beast he had fought, but sadly each one of them perished horribly but fought valiantly. The creature just laughed as it stood high and prideful. Typhus slowly stood to his feet.

"You will not get what you came for, you abomination!" Typhus spat on the ground then cursed.

"We shall see." The creature turned to where the bright ball of light was making his way over to it. Scar rushes to Typhus.

"I'm fine. Go!" He nodded.

"I'll take him on and defeat him!" Rushing to cut the beast off, Scar stood in front of his path.

"Move out of my way, little pest!"

"I have no time for it to be wasted upon you." Montorious grew impatient. The monster then squinted his four upside-down triangle-shaped eyes at Scar. "Take your forces and leave this place and never come back, and I might let you live." Scar grinned.

"*Ha! Ha!* You fool. I am a supreme commander in one of the greatest Armies known to man, who serves the mightest being on this wretched planet. The great Montorious!" The creature stood prideful with his giant double-edged sword in one hand as his tail that was long and a giant-shaped hand at the end wielded a sword also. "Enough talk. *Fight!*"

And the beast charged Scar as he did the same. The monster twirled his double-edged sword as it clanged against Scar's sword, both of them having substantial ground and strength. The beast then swung his tail around to slice Scar in half with his sword. *Swoosh!* Scar ducked and backed up just in time, as he then pulled out a dagger from his left leg pocket and aimed for the creature's head. But he deflected it at the last second. The two once more clanged sword to sword as they both used impressive skills. *Clang! Swoosh!* Scar ducked down.

"You cannot defeat me, boy!" The creature twirled his double sword, then making some type of battle pose. Dozens of men were yelling. Scar looked behind the monster as eight more men of the kings came charging toward them.

"No!" yelled Scar.

"*Ha! Ha! Ha!* Come! Meet the same fate as your kin!" said the beast welcoming them evilly.

He fully faced the eight men approaching, completely ignoring Scar, or so he thought. Now was his chance to pierce him right into his back! He slowly stepped closer, carefully looking at his other sword that dangled from the huge beast as it swung from side to side. Men were yelling as they began to fight the beast. "Good, he's distracted," Scar whispered to himself as he then lunged to stab its back. *Clang!* His sword on his tail sensed somehow. As Scar then began fighting with the giant hand, he was shocked that the beast could continue fighting the eight opponents and use his tail to fight him so immensely. Finally, Scar had disarmed the beast's sword that the giant hand held but froze, for what he saw next was nothing he's seen before that was so gross and frightening. He squinted as the creature's hand opened up and became a giant mouth with rows of razor-sharp teeth and one oval-shaped eyeball that was red with five eyelashes. It lunged at Scar far as it could, snapping and biting ferociously, dripping some type of muck on the ground. Scar swung at it and missed! The giant hand that was also a mouth moved swiftly. It seemed impossible. Scar yelled at the remaining men to throw their spears! This would give him a chance, once he's wounded. *Swoosh! Swoosh! Clang! Clang!* The beast blocked two. "*Argh!*" But failed as he cried out to deflect the rest that pierced his body all over, stumbling back a bit.

"You shoulda took the deal," said Scar as he then sliced off the monsters giant hand off. Blood sprayed everywhere, some on Scar's face. He then jumped into the air, wasting no time. "Your tyranny has come to an end!" yelled Scar as he hoped onto the creature's chest and pierced his sword straight into his throat.

Then there was a loud thump and bang as the beast laid dead as his weapon fell beside him. The creature then became cold as ice then caught on flames spontaneously. Scar quickly pulled his sword out, then wiped it off on the fallen beast. Cheers yelled throughout the courtyard as Scar walked more away from the power source now that it was safe. He then saw a man limping, walking across the bridge. It was Kanos! He survived but was covered in blood. Scar walked over and greeted him.

"I see he didn't beat you up too bad," said Kanos.

"Surprised you made it considering how long it took," said Scar as he smiled, then Kanos as they both embraced by hugging for a split moment.

Then they both turned to look at the aftermath of the battle itself—dozens of men, monsters of Montorious, and Mandare all lied dead in the courtyard. Typhus made his way to them as he didn't say a word, just walked past with his men to go look at his distraught city. Floyd flew over to Scar and landed on his shoulder and gave each of them a short smile but that was all. They began to follow Typhus. Scout ran up to Scar and licked his hand as he simply patted his head. Finally, reaching the streets of Baltar, but it wasn't a pretty sight, a sad one indeed. Buildings were turned to ruble an on fire, but most of all, thousands of innocent people laid dead in the street, piled along with more of Typhus's soldiers. Typhus fells to his knees.

"My lord," one soldier said.

"So much death." Typhus looked around sad from both fronts of the many losses him and Montorious had. Scar knelt down where Typhus was and looked out in pity.

"Surely with all this might, power can be such a curse," said Scar as he looked deep into Typhus's eyes seeing much pain as he did as well, and as the smoke arose over Baltar, everything was silent, and if you were there, you could feel all the pain and the many souls of the dead.

CHAPTER 7

Can the Dead Come Back to Life?

Scar slowly helped Typhus off his knees as his soldiers began walking around cleaning up the city using magic to rebuild the broken walls and buildings. Townspeople walked around crying, yelling out for loved ones. Kanos helped an elderly woman with her things. "Have you seen my grandson?" she asked with tears forming in her eyes. "I must find him." She started to walk away talking to herself. Typhus turned over a table in anger as Scar then laid a hand upon his shoulder.

"Typhus, I understand your pain, but now we must talk about the next move." Typhus took a deep breath.

"You're right." He nodded. "Come. Let us go back to my castle for a drink."

He walked past a dead body growing sad in his eyes yet again. Kanos and Floyd stayed behind to help rebuild Baltar as Scout followed Scar. Walking over the bridge now, Typhus makes his way through the courtyard to the gate glancing at the bright ball of light. "Good. Still safe," he muttered. Typhus walked into his castle and kept walking and made a right into a different room with all his friends that had survived the battle. Arguing among themselves soon as Typhus walked in it stopped as everyone bowed. Scar saw familiar faces, some not too happy to see. Typhus sat, and everyone did the same.

"What of my queen?"

"She's safe, my king," one said. Typhus nodded as it seemed a huge weight was lifted from him.

"So what's the next move?" asked Typhus to his fellow friends and highest in command.

"I say we take the fight to Montorious now! Make him pay for what he's done."

"No, you fool!" another yelled. "We will be annihilated! We should just stay here an let it all pass on its own."

"No!" yelled another.

"*Silence!*" yelled Typhus, as he balled up his hand into a fist and slammed it down on the table. His men became quiet, then looked toward him. "What do you propose?" asked Typhus, now looking at Scar.

"We continue to rebuild your city and after, prepare for war, gather everyone, load up ships, and make our way to Kasanaski Mountain. My other allies around the world are probably almost there. We are the last," Scar said strongly. Typhus thought for a moment.

"Yes! We shall do that," he said triumphantly.

"But there's one other matter we must take care of." Typhus's men, whispered among themselves knowing.

Scar made a puzzled look and asked, "What?"

"Come," said Typhus. "Follow me, and you shall see." He walked out the room, and his men quickly followed as did Scar and Scout. Returning back outside near the giant ball of light. They all gathered around it.

"My lord! Look." Everyone gasped.

"Impossible!" Typhus cursed. Looking closer, he saw a piece of his power source missing! "Find the thief. Bring them here! Go!"

"It's Scar, your majesty!" Aphemis pushed people aside and pointed angrily.

"That's a high accusation to make." Typhus looked over at Scar. "He was near me most of the time. It cannot be him."

"His friends must have then!" Aphemis yelled.

"No! No!" Scar yelled back.

"They're helping rebuild the city!"

"*Lies!*" Aphemis drew his sword, but people held him back.

"Zahem! Ramos!" Typhus yelled. "Find me this thief."

"Yes, sir!" And all of Typhus's headmen left, some dragging Aphemis away as he yelled and cursed, trying to break free. Typhus then began what he was trying to do at first. He pulled out just a handful of mana light as it shone blue and black.

"Whoa," Scar said in awe as he stepped in closer to observe more. "What are you going to do?" Scar asked. Typhus smiled.

"Follow me." He left the area and walked back into his castle all the way back into the giant patio that overlooked the entire city. Scar watched as Typhus closed his eyes and raised up both his hands as he opened them wide. His eyes shone a bright light and with dozens of purple specs in each eye that moved frequently like a gas state. Dozens of medium-sized balls of blue mixed with black light portrayed out and dispersed among the city. It was truly a marvelous sight. By this time, Scar had an idea of what was happening, for Typhus was bringing the dead back to life. It progressed for about thirty-five minutes until Typhus took a knee, for it was done. Sweating, taking deep breaths, as Scar helped Typhus to his feet.

"You brought them back, didn't you?" Scar had a shocked look on his face but then smiled.

"Yes. Yes, I did, for the power that lies in Baltar is magnificent. But bringing people back to life that had just died can only be done once. It heals them completely, fixes all their wounds. Sadly, some I could not saved, for they died in ways that are irreversible," said Typhus. "So that's why I was so sad, for if we're attacked again, I won't be able to bring them back."

"Well, but at least you've given them a little more time with their loved ones if so," Scar said, trying to be positive.

"I just wish it'd all never happened, but"—Typhus sighed—"what's done is done." Scar looked down in sadness. "But we shall rejoice! Many people are back!" Typhus yelled out happily. Scar's heart quickly dropped.

"But what of you know whose forces?" asked Scar worried.

"They're being disposed of now into a huge pile and burned," Typhus said harshly.

"My lord! My lord!" A soldier came rushing toward Scar and Typhus as he knelt before the king.

"What is it?" Typhus asked confused and interested. Heavy breathing, catching of breath. "Take your time, son," said Typhus.

"We…we've captured one. One of the thieves!"

"There's more?" said Typhus angrily. "Show me where! They will pay dearly for this treason." Typhus then rushed off the patio.

"Yes, my king!" the man said fearfully as they both fast passed walked.

Scar was running behind, trying to keep up. Making their way to the middle of the courtyard where the accused supposable thief was on their knees with a bag over their face. They were surrounded by soldiers and Typhus's head people. Typhus rushed over and lifted off the bag from the accused person. He gasped. "It cannot be," said Typhus. Scar's face grew big in astonishment, and his heart dropped in sadness, for it was Telina, the servant girl he admired. "Why, you have the audacity! To come into my kingdom and do such a treacherous act!" Typhus then drew his sword from one of his men. Telina cried.

"No!" yelled Scar as he ran past people and pushed them out the way, but Aphemis put out his arm an knocked him down, putting his big boot over Scar's cheek.

"Stay down, boy," he said angrily as he then gave a crooked smile.

"Typhus!" Scar yelled. Typhus raised the sword high into the air about to take the life from her. "Wait! At least hear why she did it," Scar pleaded.

"So much death already has been shed. But brought back!" Aphemis yelled, stating as he pressed his boot down harder upon Scar's face. Sword clanged to the ground as Typhus took a deep breath and calmed down. "You're right. Aphemis! Release him!" Typhus turned, giving a deep stare into his eyes.

"Yes, my king." Aphemis pressed down hard with his boot upon Scar's face before lifting up, leaving a burn and a mark.

"Help her up!" Typhus yelled, while another quickly untied the rope binding her wrists. "Speak, Telina." Typhus tried to tone down his extreme anger, sniffling, wiping of face.

"Jasper, my brother, and I came here to take some of your power source to save our family an friends that were taken by Montorious." Men whispered among themselves.

"She's lying!" yelled Aphemis. Typhus then gave Aphemis a look as he then didn't say a word.

"Go on, Telina."

"Montorious said he'd set them free if we did this task."

"Why'd he want it in the first place?" asked Scar, curious and demanding as he walked closer to where Typhus stood.

"He needs it," said Telina. "For it will provide the necessary energy to apply his supernatural strength ability."

"How do we not know all this time you and your deceitful brother haven't been taking our power source since you've been here? Who knows how many evil powers she's helped him gain," said Aphemis, looking at Telina angrily.

"No! No! I promise this is the first time!" Telina said while fear began to grow in her voice. Typhus's eyes grew big as one of his men spat on the ground.

"That actually sounds like something deranged he'd attempt on himself. But what of your brother, Jasper?" asked Typhus. "Where is he? Where is the power source?" he yelled growing angry once more.

"He must have took it. I hid it somewhere he wouldn't find it to return it later. He must have followed me," Telina said, trying not to tear up. "He must have left hours ago along with it. I chose to stay behind after I knew what we planned was wrong. Also so I could tell you and ask if you could possibly help me get my family."

"I think we should help," said Scar aloud. "And in the long run, stop Jasper from giving that power source to Montorious, of course."

"Agreed," said Typhus, "but you shall go, Scar, and take some of my men with you." Typhus stared at Scar. "I've known you a bit now and fought with you. I know I can trust you with this task." Scar nodded. "Come!" Typhus yelled. "We must move quickly. Zahem! Ramos! you will accompany Scar to find Jasper as well as two squads of my men. Who knows what evil lies ahead."

"Yes, sir!" They both rounded up twelve men each. "And two Mandare also. Now!" Typhus pointed at Telina. "You shall go as well. Maybe you can reason with your brother."

"Yes, sir." She walked away to go grab some belongings.

"Kanos and Floyd come into the courtyard."

"What's going on?" asked Kanos as he watched many men packing things up.

"We're leaving," said Scar. "I'll tell you as we gather our stuff." Kanos nodded.

Now that everyone was situated, they all went aboard Scar's ship and set a course to the next town over. Men rushed to find a room as Scar's robots walked around taking care of what needed attending. As the ship pushed its way out the harbor into the open sea furthering its distance, you could no longer see the ship if you were in Baltar. The sky began to be covered in gray as cumulonimbus clouds blanketed the sky. Ramos looked out to sea on the top back deck.

"So you think will find this guy?" asked Zahem as he approached Ramos from afar. He, too, then looked out and stared boldly into the endless sight of water.

"I don't know. I fear—" And before he could finish his sentence, Scar approached them.

"Of course, we will," said Scar in a confident voice as he somehow heard the entire conversation. The two said nothing but looked down. "We must!" Scar gave the two a serious stare and then walked away.

Rain began to fall while Scar went to his room to rest his eyes for a bit. The rain poured down hard like a plague. Thunder and lighting struck the sky repeatedly. The ship swayed back an forth as Scar had trouble sleeping. So instead, he lay on his back as he stared up at the ceiling, thinking of all the tiresome events he's been through. "Why'd this happen to me?" he asked himself. He could have avoided all this if he'd just never gone on vacation and went to that small island to then face an unexpected numerous amount of foes and stumble upon a tribe. He told a man there he'd want to stop this unknown superb foe, which now he felt stupid for saying since he new vaguely about him. But Scar then felt bad, for he knew that a true warrior, or good man would not just sit back and just let evil prosper so great. He knew that he had to put a stop to this man. Scar then heard loud yelling on the top deck as he jumped out of bed and threw his cloak on as he then rushed out the door up the stairs.

"Scar!" yelled Kanos.

"We're close to the next town. It'll take us a day to get there through the way this storm is," replied Scar. A soldier grabbed a pair of binoculars. "Ramos!" he yelled.

"What is it?" Ramos rushed over to see what was wrong as the rain constantly poured down making it hard to see. Ramos then took the binoculars from the man as he observed for a bit. "My word," said Ramos in a fearful voice. He slowly turned around as rain ran off his face as his eyes grew big. "Gandar has fallen to the enemy." Ramos was now trembling.

"Let me have a look," said Scar. Looking through to see giant fires everywhere, you could see tiny specs of men walking back and forth, guarding the wall and below creatures standing guard.

Scar handed a soldier the binoculars. "Rest good tonight, men. We go to battle tomorrow and take back Gandar." Scar turned and looked at the pillaged town. "Jasper is hiding somewhere in there. I'm sure of it."

All the men dispersed. The storm finally ceased as everyone was peacefully resting. Morning came swiftly as the skies were covered in fog. Scar got up and put on his weapons as he made his way to the top deck. He then went to go talk to his robot that was steering the ship. "Take us near the side of the wall." Kanos came up the stairs. "I'll move some of the fog so we may see our way and move the fog toward are enemy so they won't see us coming." Kanos closed his eyes as they turned gray and white as he stepped back down the stairs near the side of the ship, putting both hands up as high winds began to move the fog. The ship pressed closer to the town being undetected as the robot put the ship carefully near the side of the wall.

"Men gear up an get ready." Scar walked down the steps to greet his men. "All right," said Scar as he tried to talk as low as possible. "Ramos, you'll take your squad to the right when we're over the wall." He nodded. "Zaheem, the left, and mine will go through the middle. Find Jasper, capture him alive." Scar looked at the Mandare. "When we start fighting, you guys then come join the fight. For now, watch the skies for us." The two Mandare made an unusual noise, but it seemed they acknowledged.

Scar pulled out his remote. He swiped through the hologram and pulled out grappling hooks for everyone except for Kanos as he just flew over the wall to see if the coast was clear. *Whoosh!* Kanos stepped on the wall and looked in every direction, while men walked past as some Kadaki fire spitters trickled behind them. Then they were out of sight. Kanos then waved his hand to signal the coast was clear. *Clink! Clink! Clink!* Dozens of grappler hooks swung over the wall as all the men, including Scar, began climbing up the rope rising high to the top of the wall. They all then went down the other side gingerly then split into their groups. Floyd flew over the wall and perched on Scar's shoulder.

"Almost left without me," Floyd whispered.

"Quiet," said Scar as he led his men past a house, while they all stepped very cautiously waiting for the proper time to attack.

Scar continued to walk leading his team as they hid behind numerous houses as air donos posted up on higher houses. Their eyes were as sharp as needles, trying to see if anyone tried escaping from Gandar. Dozens of giant crabs Scar saw from afar now began to emerge from the other side of town guarding that area. Scar then cursed.

"I think now we're outnumbered," he whispered to Floyd.

"When are we not?" replied Floyd as Scar ignored his smart remark.

"Okay, let's move," said Scar as they carefully ran to the other side half across the street, surprisingly all but one.

Men waved their hand mouthing, "Let's go. You can do it." But the soldier froze. He couldn't. While Scar's squadron dealt with the issue, he went ahead a bit more. Scar reached the corner of a house as he slowly peeped his eye out to see four men and two Kadaki fire spitters. But wait! Scar saw a fifth man approaching. It was Jasper! Jasper laughed greeting the other men.

"So let's see it one more time!" one of them yelled.

"All right. Shut up!" said Jasper as he reached deep into his pocket an pulled out a bright ball of light. The men squinted their eyes in amazement. Jasper put it back in his pocket.

"You should leave soon and give that to Montorious! He doesn't like to be kept waiting. Think of what he'd do to you if you lost it." The man stepped straight into Jasper's face.

"I won't." He then pushed the man back. The man quickly drew his sword. Jasper gave him a look. "We're on the same side for now." An before the man could say anything else, a loud *clang* erupted.

"What was that?" one man yelled.

"Oh no," said Scar as he rushed back to his men. Floyd flew quickly behind for the last man that was so afraid had tripped while running over, and his shield fell off his back and rolled. Air donos swooped down.

"*Attack!*" yelled Ramos from across the town, and dozens of men ran from their posts as they met Scar's units into battle. Scar turned around to go back the way he came, but he froze, for not one but two Kadaki fire spitters blocked his path. They were only five feet away. Floyd was back upon Scar's shoulder digging his claws in by fear. "Ouch! Floyd, get off me!" Scar began to sweat. The Kadaki fire spitters just growled as they blinked, and their eyes split. One tried to pounce at Scar, but he drew his sword in a slow-motion whoosh! Scar fell to the ground. And when he quickly reached for his sword, there was a Mandare standing in front of him baring that symbol he once saw. As the beast roared and formed a giant greenish-blue orb, he shot at the monster. It fell instantly in one hit. The other retreated as the Mandare ran after it. Scar quickly rose to his feet meeting his men into battle. He saw from afar all the giant crabs attack a squadron of men. "We will defeat them!" yelled Zaheem as they formed a line. "Spears!" yelled Zaheem as all the men picked up their spears. The giant crabs drew closer as the ground shook. People in their homes closed their windows. *Fire! Whoosh! Whoosh! Whoosh! Whoosh! Whoosh!*

Spear after spear flew into the air some hitting its target effectively as some giant crabs simply snapped some in two. But dozens more were still coming straight for them. Ramos's squadron were taking on Crokinians as they fought valiantly, but some perished, while Scar was back-to-back with Kanos fighting men. Swords clung together.

"Where's Jasper?" asked Kanos while swords were still clinging together.

"I'm not sure," said Scar. "Last I saw he was over there." Scar quickly pointed.

"*Go!* I'll hold them off!" Kanos then formed two ice spears as Scar ran down the narrow path to stop Jasper.

Kanos threw multiple ice spears the way he came to blockade it off. Scar ran spry down the corridor into the ship dock.

"*Jasper!*" yelled Scar as he could see him on a tiny boat drifting off to sea as he waved. And if you were with him you could see him smile manically. Scar cursed. *Roar!* as a Crokinian snuck up on Scar. *Swoosh* went an arrow right into the beast's head. *Wham!* It fell hard and laid dead. Scar looked down in awe as he was caught off guard, then looked to which direction the arrow had came from as he saw a soldier. He then nodded as he ran another way back to Kanos. It seemed the battle had ceased almost as he looked around. Only a few men and beasts still put up a fight.

"Did you get him?" asked Kanos approaching Scar from afar as he was scratched, bruised, and covered in blood smiling.

"No," said Scar while looking down in anger.

"Hey, don't worry." Kanos nodded to Scar and laid a hand upon his shoulder. "We'll get him."

"Come, let us return to the ship," said Scar. "We must quickly set a course to the direction Jasper went."

"Let's move!" yelled Kanos as Zaheem had just pierced the last foe with his sword, then rounded up his men as the others did.

"How many?" asked Scar as they were all aboard the ship leaving Gandar.

"Eight total." Ramos looked down in pity. Scar balled his hand to a fist as he slammed it down upon the ship railing. He yanked the soldier's responsible from them being caught onto the edge of the ship.

"If you hadn't been a clumsy fool! They'd still be here!"

"That's enough, Scar!" yelled Kanos firmly. Scar looked down at the terrified man as he just slowly let go of him. Kanos laid a hand on Scar's shoulder. "You can't save everyone, my friend." Kanos looked at Scar deeply. Scar turned away. "They fought with honor and the best they could. We were outnumbered. Even if the boy didn't fall, those men still would have died."

"You don't know that!" yelled Scar.

"They were nowhere near the boy when they perished. The way they fought sealed their fate," said Kanos. Scar looked down as he breathed heavily and shook his head. Then raised it again and nodded.

"I think I'll lie down for a while. Tell the robot these coordinates." Scar wrote them down on a piece of paper an handed it to Kanos.

"I got it covered," said Kanos as he walked away.

Scar then walked to his room all gloomy. Floyd flew over next to Scar but didn't say anything. Scar then reached to open his door as Scout greeted him happily. Scar smirked. "Missed you, too, boy." He looked at Floyd, who was still outside his door flapping his wings, staring at him, blinking his three eyes. Scar waved his hand for him to come in. He then walked over and shut the door. He then walked to his fridge and grabbed a drink, then sat down as he thought about what he could have done differently to not let Jasper escape. *Gulp! Gulp! Gulp! Gulp!* He threw the can. Scar laid his head down to rest and hoped to be free from all these tiresome feelings of stress. Scout and Floyd fell asleep as Scar eventually did also as the three slept peacefully until there was a knock on the door. Scar wiped his eyes as he rose out of the bed.

"Who is it?" asked Scar as he walked to the door and opened it. His eyes grew big and surprised. "Telina?" He began to shut the door in anger.

"No. Wait. Please, Scar." She put her foot in the door. "I came to apologize," said Telina. Scar then studied her for a moment as he let her in.

"Sit," said Scar as he pulled up a seat for her.

"Thank you," said Telina as Scar had walked to the end of the room and looked out the window. "Scar, I'm sorry for not telling you sooner about what my brother and I had planned to do."

"Yes," said Scar. "You forgot to mention you're a thief and a liar." Telina then stood up.

"I did what I thought was right!" yelled Telina.

"Well, evidently, it wasn't!" yelled back Scar. He then looked Telina in the face as she began to cry. She sat back down. Scout trotted over to her and nudged her leg.

"Don't be so hard on her," said Floyd in a low voice.

"But she's a liar an—" Scar stopped himself as he sighed and looked at Floyd, then made his way to Telina. "I'm sorry," said Scar as Telina slowly lifted her head up.

"You have no idea what he's like. I've seen terrible things done to those I care about. Montorious," Telina said lividly, "is evil!" Scar reached out his hand, then hesitated, then casually put his hand on hers.

"We'll get your family and friends back. I promise." Scar smiled, while she then wiped her face from tears. Scar could now see her beautiful bright-green eyes shine in a way, glistening as the light from the moon shone in. Telina smiled back as she said okay and put her other hand upon Scar's. Scar smiled once more. Yelling up on the top deck, Scar removed his hand quickly as he rushed out the door to the top deck.

"What's going on?" Scar said demanding.

"It's Jasper!" yelled a soldier, pointing out to where the ship was headed.

"Impossible!" said Scar. "We shouldn't be this close to him already, but how?"

"The ice," said Kanos as he pointed out. Scar hadn't realized that they were in an entirely different place where there were giant icebergs.

"Hurry up. We must catch up!" pleaded Scar.

"We can't," said Ramos approaching.

"The ice is slowing us down. Looks like it did for Jasper as well," said Zaheem smirking.

"But he can hear us. Look out!" yelled a soldier as Jasper had detonated a bomb on one of the icebergs. A big explosion erupted as ice chunks fell off the forty-five-foot berg onto the ship as well as hitting pieces that had fallen into the water. It pushed them off course from Jasper.

"No!" yelled Scar. "Turn this ship around! *Jasperrr!*" yelled Scar.

"It's too late. We're being pushed further out," said a soldier as it began to snow hard, and the winds became high, blowing people to the ground. Kanos tried to calm the winds down a bit. The ship swayed back and forth as the robot manning the ship finally took her steady. The ship pushed with ease now through the icy waters. Scar looked as it's still snowing.

"Scar!" yelled Floyd as he flew toward him, Scout and Telina followed as well. "What happened?" yelled Floyd. Scar slowly turned his head to face Floyd.

"He got away," Scar said in a livid voice.

Telina walked beside Scar an asked, "Are you all right? Scar took a moment to respond, trying to change his attitude.

"I'm fine," Scar stated as Telina gave a slight smirk as if what he said wasn't true.

"I love my brother, but it seems he's changed completely. I don't know him." She looked down. "Do what you must," said Telina in a sad voice as she looked down. Scar looked at Telina, then upon a man simply passing by that stopped to look into the water. He leaned over further to take a closer look.

"What is that?" The soldier asked aloud seeing only chunks of ice now floating in the water. As he lifted his head back from over the side of the ship, he began to turn around. But not even two feet away, a creature yanked him off the ship as he yelled. *Splash!* Scar stood up as he looked in awe, for it had happened so quickly, he couldn't react fast enough.

"Men!" yelled Ramos. "Draw swords!" Scar deployed more robots from his device as well. The creature then emerged sprouting out of the water, slamming onto the deck, holding the man in his hand as he then held him out, just staring upon everyone on the ship. Unfearfully, it said not a word.

"Let him go!" Scar yelled, then told Telina to get below the bottom deck as Scar then drew his sword and waved his hand for her to go. The creature then threw the man hard into another soldier as he coughed hard shaking dripping water. The beast then stared at Scar angrily dripping water from its body, having one giant eyeball as the outside was oval shaped and in the inside was diamond shaped. It had eyebrows as well that looked like jagged razors, covered in frost as he had giant spikes that covered both arms in one row and two giant spikes above each shoulder. It had pointy dagger feet. It then roared a disturbing unusual sound as you could see it slightly smirk as dozens more like him sprouted out of the water all around them, having weapons of many varieties. Mandare formed energy balls, ready to attack. The creature that seemed like the boss raised up his hand as he balled up his fist. At that moment, they attacked swiftly and surprisingly with much skill. Scar charged the head monster yelling.

"*Stop!*" an anonymous person said as Scar was puzzled and looked to see a tall-figured man in a hood approach him as the creatures fell back to him as he walked past them slowly. And as he took off his hood, Scar looked in awe and dropped his sword, for he had seen an old friend.

CHAPTER 8

The Return of the Lost Soldier

The man laughed as Scar slowly walked closer to him. "You… you died." Scar was still so astonished, for it was Adam. Man sighed.

"I thought so as well." Scar was now standing in front of Adam. "After you left, it seemed as if they just kept coming, endless waves of men and monsters. I was so weak, so I had remembered about my hidden tunnel I had made under my beach. I made my way to it as I went below without being seen. From all the fire and smoke, I doubt they spotted me." Adam smiled. "After that, I took my boat and went off to find you, but instead, I journeyed much further in the opposite direction. I showed up here." Adam looked up and around. "I was freezing, nearly felt like I was dying when these beasts"—Adam put his hand on one—"surprisingly saved me, got me well. Told them later my story and who I was on a quest to take out. They happily agreed to help me. They don't care for that mad man. Anyways, I planned to leave here with them to join you at you know who's castle with"—Adam raised his hands—"reinforcements."

"Well, it's good to know you're alive." Scar sighed. "I went to a dark point, thought the worse." Adam put his hand upon Scar's shoulder.

"I'm here now, my friend." He nodded. "So what brings you out here?" Adam grew excited. "Is it finally time?"

"Unfortunately, not." Scar grew disappointed. "We came out here chasing someone. Have you seen anyone else out here?" asked Scar.

"No," said Adam. "If anyone was here, they're long gone now. Once you enter these parts, you're practically like a ghost. There's nothing out here anyway."

"No, you're wrong. Kasanaski Mountain is where Montorious is." Adam's eyes grew big.

"But that's just a two-day journey from here." Scar looked in awe for a moment.

"But come! Let us sit back and relax like the good old days and discuss this."

"Why, of course!" said Adam as he spoke in a different language, and the ice creatures dispersed back into the icy waters.

"Men! it's okay! Go back to your usual duties." Men dispersed. "You'll have to stay here for the night. It'll take the Iendu awhile to make a path from which you came. The icebergs are treacherous." Scar waved his hand.

"Not a problem."

The two sat down as Scar then told about who he met and his dangers along the way. They ate, drank, and laughed, like they did back on Adam's oasis island. The snow continued to fall but settled down and began to float down gingerly. Floyd flew over to Scar. *Brrr!* He shook off his wings.

"I hate this place!" complained Floyd. "It's too cold." Adam laughed.

"Well, we'll be leaving soon and on our way back to Baltar," replied Scar.

"Well, good! Sooner the better," said Floyd as he then flew off somewhere else. Adam laughed again.

"Your friend is such a character, isn't he?" Scar covered his face with his hand.

"Gosh, that bird."

"So Baltar?" Adam asked seeming interested.

"Baltar is where the last of my forces that joined me stay," said Scar. "A king named Typhus rules there. His unique friends are over there." Scar tilted his head as Adam's eyes became wide, not having the chance to gaze upon them till now. "They're called Mandare," Scar said smiling. "And you should see them in their other forms."

"Other?" Adam now looked at the beasts even harder, more intrigued.

"You'll see soon enough." Scar began to walk.

"Well, I'd like to come back with you to Baltar and bring my new friends."

"Why, of course," said Scar as he tried to look for an Iendu.

"No. No, not those friends." Scar now seemed now to look puzzled on his face. Adam smiled.

"Yes, I forgot to mention that many people live out here, and I've made them allies.

"I'm impressed," said Scar. "But, why, of course. You may come back with all your friends. I missed you very much so, and whoever you know must be surely good indeed!" Adam nodded.

"They'll be here by morning. I'll signal them tonight."

"How many will be coming?" Scar asked. Adam turns to face Scar.

"Five hundred men." Scar nearly choked on his drink that he was sipping.

"Five hundred!" he blurted out now smiling.

"Is there enough room?" asked Adam seeming worried for a moment.

"Of course, there is. This ship has forty thousand rooms," said Scar proudly.

"Now I'm impressed," said Adam as he smiled. "Well, we might as well get some rest," said Adam. "The Iendu should be finished then." Adam then looked over the side of the ship and saw the Iendu still slicing and removing ice.

"I'll tell my robot to begin turning us around now to save time tomorrow," said Scar as he then shook Adam's hand. "It was good seeing you again, old friend."

"As to you," said Adam as he nodded his head.

The two then went their separate ways as Scar later returned back to his room where Floyd and Scout were nestled asleep. He just smiled and walked to his window, while snow fell down still, and the stars sparkled brightly as the moon shone bright making the ice shimmer. It was a beautiful sight. Scar then sat on his bed thinking of all the previous events, excited that tons of people will be on his ship by morning, also happy his friend Adam was still alive as Scar was well as mind boggled by the creatures he met. Scar lay back down and just looked at the ceiling. He then smiled, slowly closing his eyes, dreaming happily and peacefully of things, for everything was finally coming together, and now he had his Army. The next day drew near as Scar was awoken by the sound of a large crackle as he arose out of bed and looked out the window to see a bright-red light shoot up into the sky as it began to come back down slowly. Scar fell back asleep but later awoken by Scout as he pounced on his stomach, not realizing how heavy he was. "*Uf!*" Scar rose out of bed startled. "I'm up! I'm up!" yelled Scar as he then looked at Scout who was on top of him, wagging his tail that sparked light, barking happily. "Well, we better hurry," said Floyd, "'cause we got company." Scar looked past Floyd, who was standing in the window sill to see dozens of boats approaching in the distance. Scar lifted the covers as fast as Scout hopped down off the bed as he rushed out the door to the deck. Scar could see some boats had already reached his ship as people began to board, all bundled up wearing heavy clothing. Adam went and greeted them as well as Ramos, Zaheem, and Kanos. Scar went and did the same, while he helped a man board upon the ship.

"Hello!" said the man as he nodded as did Scar.

"Welcome! Take any room you like." He pointed to the direction they were.

"Thank you, Scar. I, as do all of us, appreciate your kindness," said the man as he walked away before Scar could respond. Adam then approached Scar.

"I told them all about you, your stories, and what your journey was about." He smiled, shaking Scar's hand. Scar then put his hands up.

"I'm not all that." Scar watched to see a few more boats approaching, while people were still boarding his ship. "Start the engine! Prepare to leave," yelled Scar up to his robot.

"Don't be modest, Scar!" said Adam. "You've brought us all together." He put out his hand wide by passing people aboard the ship. Scar then looked at Adam then at the Iendu creatures that were breaking the ice as the people that were approaching were finally aboard. The ship then finally began its long voyage back to Baltar. "No one could ask anymore of you," said Adam as he looked at Scar seriously. "You decided to stop a force that you knew vaguely about at first, put yourself in a life-changing situation. You're a hero, Scar," Adam said proudly.

"Others would have done what I did." Scar walked to the front of the ship watching the sunrise and smelling the fresh cool sea water as he looked to the side of the boat and saw the Iendu swimming alongside. Adam laid a hand upon Scars shoulder.

"No they wouldn't have. Everyone was too afraid, or battling with their own tragic events as I was." Adam then looked down in sadness. Scar patted Adam on the back as he looked out to sea.

"As I left your island, I ran into some interesting forces."

"That is?" asked Adam, seeming interested.

"These ghosts that prospered in the Bonteka Lake, they called it. Taunting me about my journey and of your death, like they knew everything about me. It was weird." Adam's eyes grew big.

"Seems so." Scar looked and nodded.

"After, I got so angry. I lashed out upon one and grasped its neck somehow. How is that possible?" asked Scar. "Even they were shocked. One said aloud, 'Could it be him?'"

"What you make of that?" Scar awaited a response.

"I don't know," said Adam, looking as puzzled and wanting answers as Scar did. "But there is one legend," said Adam. "Those who show no fear when facing the ghosts of the Bonteka Lake survive. They feed off your pain, then drive you insane, and you kill yourself." Adam looked down. "You somehow beat them by getting your strength back, just enough to do what you did. It's never been done before. Everyone usually perishes and becomes like them.

When you were at your lowest, that gave them the ability to form into me," said Adam.

"I understand now," said Scar as he made an expression like he'd just learned something. "Well, let's just hope I don't have to meet them again." Scar gave a small smile.

"Indeed," said Adam as the two began to laugh.

While the ship was almost out of the icy waters, you could almost feel the immense change of temperature go back up to being moderately warm. Floyd flew over to Scar as Kanos followed behind.

"Scar! Come join us for a bite to eat."

"Do you two ever stop eating?" yelled Scar as he covered his face.

"You know you're hungry!" Kanos smiled.

"You must be Kanos," said Adam walking over to shake his hand.

"Why, yes." Kanos was confused not knowing him.

"Why, Scar told me about you. I'm an old friend."

"Why, of course!" Kanos now changed his expression.

"I also hear you have an extraordinary gift." Kanos grinned as he formed an ice ball.

"Well, you could say that." He then melted it and wiped his hand on his pants. "Come eat with us! And maybe you can meet Scar's girlfriend, Telina." Kanos began to tease. Scar then gave him a look as he began to look embarrassed.

"She's not my girlfriend! But I'll see if she wants to join us." Scar walked away and slightly turned the corner of his eye to look back, still embarrassed.

"*Right*," said Kanos as he smiled and casually turned around and walked to the other side of the deck and sat down to the great quantity of food that was already laid out from the robots.

Scar went back to his room to grab Scout, then made his way down the hall to Telina's room. He knocked on door. "Gosh, this is stupid. I should just go," Scar muttered to himself as he started to walk away while the door opened.

"Scar?" He turned around as Telina gave him a smile.

"Why, hello, Telina. I…ahem"—scratching his head—"was wondering if you'd like to join my friends and I for…er…em… lunch?" Telina blushed as she looked down, then at Scar.

"Why, I'd love to." She smiled. "Just let me go change." Scar nodded as she closed the door.

"She said yes, boy." Scar whispered low overjoyed, petting Scout as Scout barked and wagged his tail. Door opened again as Telina's hair was long and in curls. She wore a white skirt that had ruffles at the bottom and a red shirt as her bright-green eyes stood out gorgeously.

"You look beautiful." Scar smiled.

"Thank you," said Telina as they both began to walk making their way up the stairs back to the deck. As they drew closer to where Scar's friends were, Floyd smacked while he stuffed his face, then briefly looked up in awe.

"Wow," he said as food fell out his mouth.

"What's up?" asked Kanos as him and Adam were confused.

They then looked in his direction as they, too, were in awe as Scar and Telina were finally to them. Adam and Kanos stood up out their chairs as they both rushed so quickly, their chairs fell back. Scar covered his face as he and Telina sat down, while Telina just laughed while Scar's friends pulled themselves together. Telina blushed once more as everyone began eating, laughing, and talking about numerous things. The sun shone bright as birds flew through the air, singing wonderful tunes. As the ship reached closer to Gandar, you could see the outskirts from afar. "You're such a pig, Floyd." Scar watched him harf down chunks of food in a matter of seconds. Everyone laughed but Scar as people gathered where they were, and they began to set up things.

"What's this?" asked Scar.

"I hope you don't mind. My friends wanted to put up a party of dancing and such." Scar waved his hand in the air.

"Not at all, my good friend." Scar looked to the side of the ship as the Iendu began to board.

"Supposedly wanting to see the party as well," said Kanos aloud as he pointed near Scar's direction.

The evening came fast as the festival upon Scar's ship that Adam's friends conducted lasted for hours, this giving more time for Scar to know Telina better as they both enjoyed themselves and walked to the back of the boat. The sun slowly set, then went down, and the moon came out.

"What a time, huh?" Scar asked Telina smiling.

"Yes, I've really enjoyed myself. I wonder also what's to happen to me next after we reach Gandar, and the final trip to Baltar is ahead. King Typhus will not be pleased to hear we failed." Telina looked down in sadness. "What will become of me? I know he has not forgotten that it was I and my brother that gave his power source to Mon—" Scar stopped her there.

"Typhus is a good man. I know he wouldn't take it out on you. You sacrificed a lot, and you've atoned for your mistake. And decided to come willingly with us to stop your brother, even if he did get away. I'll protect you from whatever happens when we get back." Scar looked into Telina's eyes seriously. She then smiled at Scar, as she reached out and touched his hand. She looked into his eyes and leaned in and kissed him. Scar was shocked, as he then smiled and looked down, then at her. "Well, we better get some rest. Have a long day tomorrow." He stood up an awaited for her.

"Like every other day," said Telina as she stood up and laughed as the two walked to the ship's rooms. Scar had walked Telina to her room as he took one last look at her beauty. She then closed the door. While he walked back to his room, leading more apart their separate ways. He went into his room, cleaned himself up, and went to the fridge to grab a drink. He then just sat on his bed thinking of Telina.

"Looks like you had a fun night," said Floyd as he was perched in Scar's window.

"You could say that." Scar smirked. Floyd cleaned his feathers.

"Well, just be cautious. She could be trying to get close to you, just to make you get your mind off what her real plan could be." Scar gave Floyd the look.

"Stop right there. She's nothing like that." Floyd flew into the room.

"I used to be on you know who's side. He has many tricks and people who are good at disguises."

"And you must be an expert then, huh?" asked Scar angrily.

"If you—" Scar stopped him there.

"I've heard enough!" he yelled throwing a pillow toward Floyd but missed, and hit Scout, who was sleeping, let out a loud woof.

"Sorry, boy." Scar then took one last look at Floyd. "Will talk more about this in the morning, but you're wrong about her. I'm sure of it," he said, laying his head down and began to slowly drift into a deep slumber.

"I hope so," said Floyd as he blinked his three eyes repeatedly and covered his face with his wings and began to sleep.

The next morning was welcoming as the sun shone bright into Scar's room beaming upon his face, waking him up. Scar stretched as he looked around the room to see Scout still sound asleep as his tail sparked light, but he didn't see Floyd. He looked to the window that was open. As Scar got out of bed and washed his face, he made his way to the door. "Come on, boy!" he shouted opening the door. Scout ran past his legs. Scar made his way up the stairs to the deck to see Adam and Kanos doing some target practice with bows and arrows. They shot arrows at stuff-filled people with hay. Well, as dart boards. *Swoosh!* "Nice shot!" Kanos patted Adam on the back. Scar walked to the side of the ship and looked out. Floyd looked at Scar from up top of the roof of the ship as he flew down on the railing beside him. The ship reached Gandar. You could see people waving from afar as the ship went by while others were rebuilding what needed tending. Scar waved back as he then noticed Floyd next to him.

"So you still thinking erratic?" asked Scar as he looked out watching the Iendu search for food.

"It's the truth, Scar," said Floyd as he blinked his three eyes, and his scorpion tail twitched.

"We will see. As for now, drop the matter, my friend."

Scar walked away to watch his friends practice shooting arrows. He greeted them, then saw a table to the right piled with breakfast. You could see the steam rise as everything looked so tasteful. There was eggs, bacon, ham, toast, hash browns, grits, pancakes, waffles, and lots of fruits and juices to drink. Scar sat down and made himself a plate as others did aboard his ship. Many formed the table longer so everyone could talk and just relax, for it was a beautiful day, while others simply slept in, worked out, or trained. Zaheem and Ramos approach Scar.

"Ah! My fellow comrades." Scar stood up and shook their hands as he then pointed down. "Eat with me!" The two sat grabbing a plate. "So we're almost back to Baltar," said Ramos as he piled his plate with food.

"Yes, but not for long, only to gather our king an the rest of our Army," replied Zaheem as he drank some of his wine.

"Yes, but will Typhus be ready?" asked Scar he may not be in his right mind to lead his troops into war. Zaheem and Ramos looked at each other.

"It is not our place to question our king's authority, even if that may be so," said Ramos as he stuffed his face with eggs.

Scar then gave a look. He then nodded. As the evening drew near, the three sat for hours simply talking getting to know one another. Zaheem and Ramos told stories of their travels in life and of other wars they've been in an witnessed but never gone up against a foe as fearfully known till now. Scar also showed them his unique device he created that took many years to complete to be perfect. The two were astonished. They'd never seen anything like it.

"That will surely come in handy when the time comes," said Zaheem as Scar pressed a button, and dozens of holograms popped out.

"It already has been." Scar smiled. While Kanos an Adam approached them, they, too, told stories and asked questions.

"Scar, are you sure your forces will come aid us?" asked Zaheem. Before Scar could answer, Kanos interrupted.

"Of course, they will because my father and tribe are one of them, and my father is no coward." Zaheem put his hands up.

"I meant no disrespect."

"None taken," replied Kanos. "My brother Rolan's tribe shall be ready as well. And the people of the lost village."

"The Hemanda," said Scar. "They have very unusual but interesting powers." Scar smiled. "That wolf I have"—he pointed—"was given to me as a gift. You should see them at their full size. It's intense." Everyone looked at Scar in awe but Kanos.

"Yes, and took us a lot of convincing to do," said Kanos.

"Well, let's just hope they stick to their word. We need every bit of help," said Adam. Floyd flew over.

"Yes, you will, for I've seen his numerous creations in incubators. He's cloned dozens of the same creatures, and it won't matter if you destroy the first one created, for he made it possible for them not to be linked. You think you've seen his worst creations already?" Floyd lowered his head down in shame. "You have no idea what awaits you on that final day when all of you are together, and you see his infinite Army of creatures. You haven't even encountered things that'd make you die where you stand. Just by looking at them would give you such a deep chill. You'd freeze and drop your weapons." Everyone was silent. Kanos took a deep breath.

"Well, jeez, Floyd, way to make the day all intense." Kanos tried to uplift the mood. Scar laughed.

"Yeah, Floyd, but we do appreciate the intel." But Floyd didn't say a word. Something else caught his gaze. He stood like a statue.

"Whoa! Floyd!" Kanos stood up. "What's wrong?" The others stood up slowly to look upon what Floyd was gazing upon, for it was a huge storm cloud in the middle of the sky and thunder and lighting that struck out of it.

"It's unnatural."

Zaheem stepped closer to see as the ship edged further to this seemingly deceitful thing. They all drew their swords but one his bow an arrow. The ship now passed under the huge storm cloud as they all looked up, and the cloud burst and spontaneously changed into fog as it swept the deck like a plague. Loud laughter. Scar's eyes grew big.

"Scar!" yelled Kanos.

"I know," said Scar as he cursed. "They're back." As fog rushed in between their legs, they could no longer see each other. Ghosts began to shimmer in an out of the fog, some different looking than Scar had last seen. Loud evil laughter.

A chill began to run down Scar's back as something whispered in his ear, "I told you, boy, you were going to die." The ghost then reached out his hand and scratched Scar's back slowly.

"No fear. No fear," Scar mumbled to himself constantly.

The fog began to slightly dissipate, just enough for Scar to see his comrades a bit.

"You're such a fool, boy!" a ghost yelled as it shimmered directly in Scar's face.

"How did you find me? How was it possible for you to leave the Bonteka Lake?" All the ghosts laughed, as the head ghost that gave Scar an evil look last time they spoke.

"You have no idea what the Bonteka Lake's power is truly capable of!" The ghost then backed away from Scar.

"We go where death is." The ghost spontaneously appeared right behind Scar. He smelled him and breathed heavily. "And you are ripe with it," said the ghost grinning wide, showing his rows of razor-sharp teeth.

"Be gone, you! Take your pathetic followers with you!" yelled Ramos as he pointed his sword at a ghost. It then bared its teeth as Ramos then sliced through it. But it simply reformed itself and laughed as it mocked him.

"We will be there when you go to war with Montorious." The sky crackled thunder as lighting shot out from the sky, and the ship shook at the mention of his name. "And we will take all the dead"—the ghost raised his hands—"back with us."

"The people that fall that day don't deserve to have to be with such evil things as you," said Scar.

"Agreed," replied Zaheem as he spat on the deck. The ghost laughed.

"It doesn't matter. They come with us anyway, but once they're at the Bonteka Lake, they can't be apart from us. And I'll see you again soon, Scar." The ghost's eyes turned red as he gave an evil smile as the fog began to rise up back to the sky.

"No, you won't." Scar squinted his eyes back at the ghost. Ghosts shot up into the sky with the fog, while the head ghost just stared at Scar and gave him a look one last time.

"Yes, I will." he then poofed into dark auroa as the fog lifted him up into the sky. The fog was gone as the sun came out, for it was the next morning.

"Whoa!" Adam made a shocked expression.

"What just happened? Floyd!" yelled Scar as he reached out his hand to touch him, but he suddenly unfroze and shook his head.

"I... I don't know what came over me. Must have been in shock."

"Well, it was a long night," said Ramos. "I think we should all get some rest and talk about this later today. We've reached Baltar almost as well. Ramos pointed from afar.

"You're right," replied Scar. "Men, get some rest."

They all dispersed. Scar opened his door as he was greeted by Scout. Scar just pat him on the head as he sat on his bed and didn't say a word. Floyd flew into his room from the window. Scar got up as he shut the window, then went back to his bed and laid his head down on his pillow as he kicked off his shoes. Scar was exhausted, and he felt so tired of all the responsibilities he now had, and the evil that had formed into the world. He just wanted to give up, even though deep down, he knew he couldn't, for it was his destiny. As the day went by, Scar was awakened by a loud rutting sound. He rose out of his bed and looked outside the window.

"Well, I'll be. We're back in Baltar," said Scar happily as he took a few minutes to get freshened up. He got dressed and left his room in a hurry with Scout. Scar ran up the stairs quickly as he was greeted by his friends, including Zaheem and Ramos.

"Ah! Just in time, Scar. We were just about to leave without you to see king Typhus!" said Adam as he put his arm around Scar.

"And no one decided to wake me?" Scar shoved Adam fooling around.

"What about me?" Floyd swept down, nearly almost swatting Zaheem in the face with his scorpion tail.

"Watch it!" yelled Zaheem, giving an unpleasant look toward Floyd.

"Good. We're all here now!" said Scar. "Let's go."

They all traveled through the busy streets of Baltar seeing that it was restored to its former glory. They edged past stores, food stands, and such as they went across the bridge, headed for the main gate. "Halt! Oh, why, it's Scar," a soldier yelled. Wave of hand. "Let them through!" They all entered the main hall. There from afar sitting on his throne was Typhus, happily seeing his new friend Scar as well as two of his headmen safely returned.

"Welcome back!" shouted Typhus as he stepped down from his throne, leisurely stepping down the steps. He raised his hands, while they all drew closer to Typhus. The king approached Scar first as Scar slightly bowed as Typhus shook his hand and his friends.

"My king," said his two headmen as they knelt down.

"Rise!" They did so.

Typhus then turned and began to walk. "So tell me! Where is Jasper? Is he still among on your ship captured?" asked Typhus overjoyed. "Where is my power source?" They all made their way to his huge patio.

Scar took a deep breath then exhaled as he then spoke, "We lost him, Typhus, through the arctic waters. He'd detonated a bomb on a berg, and we went off course." Typhus just looked out upon his city as he balled up his hand to a fist.

"Then we have a problem," said Typhus calmly as he then turned to face everyone. "Montorious now has his super strength!" Typhus became out of breath, breathing heavily. "I'm sorry." Typhus looked upon everyone on the patio. "It is not your fault he got away. For obvious reasons, events took place that stood in your way." None of them not saying a word. "Now! We must ready my troops as do you, Scar! Your forces are probably on their way there now." Scar stepped closer to which Typhus stood as he reached out his hand.

"Then we should move now," said Scar as the two shook.

"Yes!" yelled Typhus. "Ready the fleets!" Zaheem and Ramos nodded as they slightly bowed and quickly left. "Come, Scar and friends." Typhus led them off the patio as Scout and Floyd did as well. They made their way down the long hallway passing many pictures. They ran into Aphemis.

"My king, we are almost ready to leave," said Aphemis as he wore full-body armor and had many weapons on himself.

"Good!" said Typhus as he continued to proceed, but as Adam walked passed Aphemis, he stopped as the two both made an astonished look upon their faces as tears began to run down. The two hugged.

"Brother!" Aphemis tried to hold back tears. "How? I thought you perished with your family." The two stopped hugging and were five feet from one another.

"No," said Adam, wiping away tears. "I made it off in time and found my own beach." Adam began to laugh.

"Beach?" His brother began to laugh as well. "Come, you must tell me all about it!" said Aphemis overjoyed.

"Well, there's a long story." Adam smiled. Loud noise erupted as Aphemis looked up.

"It's time," he said. The two walked at a fast pace down the hall making their way to the docks to the many ships that were out in the water. Adam waved his hand.

"Come, my brother." Adam walked up a ramp. "Here's my friend's ship, Scar's!" Aphemis's eyes grew big.

"Why, of course," said Aphemis as he made his way up the ramp as they both boarded. And all the many ships pushed out to sea, and thousands of Mandare flew over head into the sky. Finally, the war was here. And the fight to Montorious was at hand.

CHAPTER 9

There Shall Be No Mercy

S car looked upon the sky, then upon the sea smiling that so many had joined the noble cause to help. He really didn't think he'd make it this far. He closed his eyes as he breathed in the fresh sea air as the sun beamed down on Scar's head. He felt life come back into him that day truly. He had his encounter with the Bonteka ghosts again. It seemed that life was slightly taken from him every time he met them but only for a period of time. Floyd flew over.

"Wonderful day, is it not?" He cleaned his feathers. Scar looked at the sky once more.

"Why, yes, it is without a doubt." Scar looked down upon the water and saw the Iendu swimming alongside. They both took a moment to admire this sensual day. While along the other side of the ship, Adam and his brother Aphemis were having a meal together talking about what they've been doing these past five months and their journeys.

"And that's how I met Scar," said Adam as he drank some of his orange juice while his brother tapped his hand on the table repeatedly. *Wham!* Aphemis then slammed his hand down.

"Brother! I don't see how you can be so happy! This man, Scar." Aphemis's eyes turned something different as his face scowled by even mentioning his name. "He hasn't done anything for you, nearly got you killed, left you there to die!"

"Brother, have you heard nothing of what I've said?" asked Adam, seeming disappointed. "I told him to go on without me."

"But it wasn't your job to protect that guy!" yelled Aphemis as he threw his glass. Aphemis said, "Adam," as he looked into his brother's eyes.

"Why is there so much anger inside of you? That was my home. It was my job to protect it and give Scar a chance to leave in doing so, for he is the resistance against"—Adam looked around—"Montorious. If he hadn't left, the rebellion against him would have never began." Aphemis looked at his brother for a moment, then turned his head in anger. He sighed.

"I'm sorry, Adam. Just when I heard word of your family, I thought the worst of you as well and broken of what happened to them too." Adam then put his head down in sadness. "But when I heard of such a terrible thing, you could have died for real this time, and the one man that could have helped you left like a coward."

Adam didn't say a word, just stared at his brother. He then sighed. "You have much to let go brother: anger, pain, hatred. Scar's a good man and friend." Aphemis then turned his head. "You just need to get to know him better. I insist," said Adam. Aphemis then looked at his brother a moment, and he then looked away.

"Well, I still believe he's working for Montorious." Aphemis tried to act like he was still mad. But he then took a deep breath as he sighed. "I will try, my brother." Aphemis slightly smiled an nodded his head.

The evening drew near as the ships made their way finally to Gandar. Some Mandare grew tired of flying, so they shape-shifted into one of two of their ground forms aboard one of the dozens of ships. Many people upon Scar's ship brought together another party. The Iendu came aboard bringing with them extravagant giant fish they'd caught and other sorts of sea creatures that were safely eatable for the festivity. There were games and dances. This also gave Scar once again time to spend with Telina, the young woman he fancied very much so. The two laughed and ate together as they were able to have their solitude, even though Floyd was that unseen pair of eyes that watched them time to time since he still didn't trust her, even though Kanos kept Floyd busy eating, of course. The festival went on for hours once more. It was a good stress reliever despite the fact the real reason why they were all coming together united. Scar looked out to the sea as if he was searching for something. Telina then put her hand upon Scar's arm.

"They'll come," she said smiling, trying to make Scar happy. He gave her a small smile as he looked out to sea again.

"I hope so," said Scar as he then turned to look at the people upon his ship that Adam had brought and some of king Typhus's men as well, then stared at a Mandare and an Iendu. Scar began talking once more. "'Cause even though it may seem we have a lot of forces, I can only imagine what awaits us when we get to—" Telina then stopped him there.

"Where is your faith, Scar?" She then looked into his eyes with her beautiful bright-green eyes staring at him. Scar just sighed.

"We're vastly outnumbered. I just know he has so many more followers."

"Wars aren't won by numbers. It comes from strategy and a plan." Telina looked at Scar feeling confident in her words. "Now I know these friends of yours will come. I believe in you and trust you, so why can't you believe in yourself? Don't let this time of tiresome evil events of trials and tribulations beat you. We're all here for you. I'm here for you." Telina then kissed Scar's cheek. "You're stronger than that." All Scar could do was smile and be amazed of how strengthening her words of wisdom were.

"Thank you for that," said Scar as he looked deeply into her eyes.

"Just doing my part." Telina smiled. While the two just laid out on the back deck all night, watching the stars that began to light up the sky, they began to close their eyes. While tiny white specs began to fall down, the ships pressed on swiftly through the sea waters now entering the icy waters, only halfway now to the inevitable fight for the world. Scar blinked his eyelashes as he slowly opened them.

Seeing a large beak and two big feet with talons on his chest, Scar then rubbed his eyes.

"Floyd? Get off me." He swatted Floyd to go away.

"Shut up and listen." Floyd's scorpion tail twitched.

"Shh." Scar put a finger to his lip. "You'll wake Telina." Scar looked at her, sleeping peacefully as she laid on her side, her back facing Scar.

"Just get up. I have something urgent to tell you." Scar gave Floyd a look as if he didn't want to while he did. He watched Floyd fly around a corner.

"Slow down!" said Scar, trying to whisper and not be any louder. Finally, Scar made it to where Floyd was as he was posted himself along the railing of the ship.

"He's here." Floyd gave Scar a deep look.

"What? Who?"

"That man you were arguing with in Baltar." Scar's eyes grew big.

"Aphemis," he mumbled as he then squinted his eyes. "But why would he choose to board my ship when he hates me?"

"Weird, I know," said Floyd. "How'd you not even see him yet?" asked Floyd. "This is your ship!" He expanded his feathers completely out.

"Quiet!" whispered Scar. He looked away to see if Telina was coming. He then faced Floyd again. "And don't get on me about that. I didn't pay attention to every person who boarded." Scar began to get mad.

"Easy, friend. I came to warn you. I think maybe he's here to kill you." Scar pondered for a moment.

"You may be right. But I'm not going to put any accusations out there." Scar then began to walk away.

"But wait," said Floyd. "That's not all." Scar froze as he then turned around. "I saw him with your friend, Adam."

"So what?" said Scar as he waved his hand and began to walk again. "Scar, listen." Scar then stopped. "He's his brother." Scar slowly turned around as his eyes grew big as he looked down.

"Brother? Adam never told me he had a brother." Scar was confused in why he never said anything, or hid it from him. "Thanks, Floyd." Scar looked up at the three-eyed bird as he nodded.

"So what are you going to do?" asked Floyd as he hopped toward Scar while still on the railing. Scar looked down, then to the sky as snow came down.

"I'm going to talk with Adam and Aphemis, and if he makes a move on me, so be it. Adam will just have to understand," said Scar as he looked at Floyd giving him a serious look. Floyd then gave one back as he nodded, while Scar then made his way to Telina as he picked her up an carried her to her room. She slightly awoke. "Go back to sleep, angel face," said Scar as he smiled and kissed her forehead. He then left the room, making his way back to Floyd.

"So yeah," said Scar now back with Floyd. "When he makes a move, I'll be ready."

"I'll watch your back," replied Floyd. Scar then nodded.

The day pressed on as many people began to walk about the ship as snow began to cease falling. The ships moved further into the icy waters, going past multiple icebergs. Scar sat on the top deck and drank a hot beverage as Scout laid by his feet, and Floyd perched himself upon his shoulder. Scar then put back his head and rested his eyes for a moment to feel the cool air blow through the air upon his face and hair.

"Look!" shouted Floyd. It nearly startled Scar so bad, he almost dropped his cup.

"What is it now, Floyd?" Scar seemed irritated. He turned his neck out to the sea. "It's a ship," mumbled Scar.

"Yes, but whose?" replied Floyd.

"Look. There's another!" yelled a soldier.

"And another!" shouted Adam as he approached.

"Everyone, be on your guard," said Scar as dozens of Mandare boarded many ships took to the sky, just in case. Multiple ships came closer to Scar's fleet.

"Draw swords!" yelled Typhus as his ship came up behind Scar's. The unknown vessels were now right upon them.

Scar pulled out his sword but then looked in awe at the man he saw across on the other ship.

"Father!" yelled Kanos as he picked up currents of wind that carried him to the other ship.

"My son!" The two embraced and hugged. It was Sepada, the chief from the first village Scar had stumbled upon, that he'd asked to join him.

The next couple of ships were different looking. They were covered in vines and had jagged giant teeth sticking out in rows. It was Nabeth! And his Army, the mighty Hemanda, came to his aid as well with their majestic Bosari wolf creatures. Scar waved as Nabeth nodded an put his hand up in the air as he balled it up into a fist. Scar was overjoyed to see him as his mind then raced, for he remembered something. If he were able to convince them to join, then Rolan would too. Scar saw three more ships come their way as thousands of men were aboard. Scar looked up on one of the decks to see Rolan wearing his long green cloak as he yelled out, "For freedom!" Everyone aboard every ship cheered. Scar sat back down to take it all in. Rolan's ship as well as the others formed a line across the water. Telina approached and sat by Scar.

"Don't say it." Scar looked at Telina, then smiled.

"Say what?"

"I told you so." Telina smiled and teased.

"I wasn't going to. I just came to see you and glad that you're happy." She laid her head on his chest, while Scar looked up too see that his ship had entered an arctic canyon.

"Fascinating." Scar leaned up to look more as the dozens of ships formed a line into the canyon.

"Scar!" yelled Adam as he waved his hand gesturing for him to come over. Scar got up.

"I'll be back." He held Telina's hand, then walked away. Greeting Adam.

"I see you've grown close to Telina." Adam smirked. Scar then smiled and turned his head back to look at her, then back at Adam nodding his head.

"Why, yes, I have. She's amazing," said Scar smiling again.

"Indeed," said Adam as he nodded, then waved his hand. "Scar, I'd like you to meet my brother." Aphemis approached, and Adam put his arm around him. Scar's eyes grew big but quickly changed back.

"Why, yes, we've met, but I didn't know this."

"Well, all that's happened, never had the chance," said Adam.

"Well, glad to see you reunited with your family." Scar nodded.

"No thanks to you." Aphemis gave Scar a look.

"Brother." Adam touched his shoulder. "Don't." Aphemis threw his hand off.

"No, Adam! This scum is a piece of crap and doesn't deserve to live. You left my brother to die!" Telina stood up, looking worried.

"It's okay." Scar saw, trying to assure her gesturing hand movements, then looked back toward Aphemis. "I didn't want to leave your brother."

"*Lies!*" Aphemis then drew his sword. Adam then fought to get it away from him.

"Stop this madness! Aphemis!" yelled Adam.

Scar then backed up, just in case. He pulled out his sword but looked down at the ground briefly to spot a weird reflection of something long and pointy. Suddenly, dozens like it appeared all over the ship. Scar looked confused.

"Look!" someone yelled as Scar looked up at the sky as dozens of arrows were in the air coming down being shot down at them.

"Telina!" Scar yelled as she was already running to Scar. He grabbed her hand, and they both ran to the bottom deck for cover, safely reaching it. "Stay here and go to your room. I will handle this." Scar then ran back up and went for cover.

"Men, draw weapons!" yelled Adam as the arrows came down. Many hid for cover, but some sadly perished as arrows rained down for fifteen minutes. They then suddenly heard the loud roar of engines overhead and shouting on the sides of the arctic canyon. Scar went out to look. He saw dozens of monsters on each side of the arctic canyon as Mandare swooped down and had already took their assault. Scar turned around to see king Typhus, and the rest of his forces were already being attacked as well, fighting for their lives.

"So it has begun," whispered a soldier that was a few feet from which Scar stood. Dozens of flying vehicles were overhead dropping men and monsters of all kinds that Scars met, but some he hadn't. Even new one's slammed upon his ship.

"No!" yelled Kanos as he'd flown back to Scar's ship from his father's, sweating as if he'd already been fighting. "That bastard Jasper! Told him we were coming!" yelled Kanos as monsters and men stormed Scar's deck as dozens more men boarded Scar's ship came up from the bottom deck to fight.

"It's an ambush!" yelled Scar as he pulled out his remote and quickly put on his armor and wielded his two swords.

More creatures climbed down from the ice canyon and jumped upon ships, some missed and fell into the icy water also from men throwing and piercing them with arrows and spears. Iendu attacked the ones that fell in keeping the fight only focused up top. Shields were shattered, monsters lost limbs, while some could blind men, then ate them. It was an all-out battle for survival, and they hadn't even made it to Montorious's fortress yet. Every step of the way, Scar felt his tyranny and his mighty wrath. But when he was fighting that day, clashing sword against sword repeatedly just after slaying a monster, or killing a man, Scar could only imagine yet again the real war that would determine the fate of the world itself. They fought for hours, it seemed. Hemanda used their physic powers to crush enemies and destroy vehicles that were in the air. Bosari hounds fought tremendously not a single one perished as their extraordinary powers were used to defeat their enemies as well. Kadaki fire spitters went head to head with Kanos as they shot out giant fireballs from their mouths. Scar battled against new forces he had never encountered before. Their body was shaped in a way of a shield as he had one giant paw with giant claws at the tip as he held a long chain with a giant spike ball at the end as his left arm seemed to be reptilian like as he had a drill for a hand. It then laughed manically.

"You're journey ends here, Scar, for Montorious grows tired of you interfering with his plans." The beast swung his spiked ball chain around. Scar ducked.

"I think not!" Yelling, trying to pierce his sword into the creature's chest, but it had no effect. It was impenetrable. "What the—" Scar backed up in awe, but the monster then lashed out with his drill. Scar put up his shield as he fell to one knee struggling to hold the shield as the drill slowly began to make its dent through.

"*Now. Goodbye, Scar!*" The beast then lifted his drill and raised his spike ball chain, and he swung it down on Scar, about to splatter him. He stopped. Scar slowly lifted his head to see that he was frozen. Kanos helped Scar up.

"Are you okay, my friend?" asked Kanos.

"Yes." Scar nodded. "Look out!" said Scar as he pushed Kanos out the way and stabbed a creature that had two heads having many eyes and two pinchers for hands.

The creature then grasped one of Scar's swords snapping it in two. Kanos quickly followed up as he brought out his two swords that lit up and became on fire as he sliced one of the pinchers off the creature, then began slicing it all over its body. The monster roared in agony and anger as fire was left where the blade had cut. The ships continued to move through the ice canyon as the battle raged on. The sky became dark gray, and snow began to fall down once more. Enemy foes fell and were tossed aside the edges of ships after being killed. Mandare fought air donos as they shot diamonds out of their tails, trying to penetrate their shells as air donos blew fire to take them out. Men in their flying vehicles shot down bombs that shook the ships leaving giant holes as Mandare attacked their vehicles and made them tumble and crash into the icy walls. Finally, the ships were almost out the deadly canyon as the fight was almost over. The beasts and men of Montorious were relentless. But one last soldier came down from a ship just before it blew up. He wore a dark-red cloak as he walked past his men and monsters that he led into battle, ignoring everything around him as he went straight for Kanos. Kanos had just slit a monster's throat. The man laughed.

"I see that you've grown stronger, little brother." The man smirked beneath his hood. Kanos turned toward the man to take a closer look as he breathed heavily, then made an upset look upon his face.

"Damion?"

"Don't be so surprised, Kanos. You knew I'd join him along with five more of our brothers."

"Five?" Kanos almost fell to his knees. "What of the others?"

"*Ha!*" The man laughed evilly. "They're prisoners now. Those fools decided to not want to be a part of our, well, his, plans." The man then smirked. "I cannot let you and your friends make it to Montorious's castle. Your quest ends here." The man formed a giant ice ball and yelled as he tossed it, then pulled out his two double-sided swords. Kanos ducked. He then charged him. *Clang!* The two collided fighting insanely.

"Don't do this, brother," Kanos pleaded aloud.

"You're on the losing side, Kanos!" The man then kicked him in his stomach. "Father never let us use our true power!" said Damion. "But with Montorious, he raises his hands, we can do anything!" Kanos shook his head.

"Brother, do you hear yourself? You sound like Zepa! And father cares about you and the rest of our brothers!"

"*Ha! Ha!*" Damion just laughed again. "That old fool? Where is he? I'll take care of him when I'm finished with you!" Damion at the moment somehow formed his two weapons into whips. They made a thunder sound every time he lashed them out. They also sparked.

"Brother, stop this madness!" yelled Kanos as he dodged a whip also from getting jolted and looked at his brother that was just laughing evilly as Kanos then shook his head. "How can you say such mindless evil things and threaten our farther?" Kanos looked down in pity and sadness. "I don't know you anymore, Damion. You're lost along with the rest of our kin, but you will surely pay for what you said about father," said Kanos as he formed two fireballs in each hand as he threw them, then his eyes turned a bright-red-orange color as he yelled and portrayed out fire from both hands six feet from which his brother stood. Damion dived out of the way as the fire then hit some of Montorious's men instead, killing them instantly.

"Join us, Kanos. Don't be a fool!" Kanos put his head down in shame.

"*No!*" he yelled as he then ran toward his brother dodging the electric whips that crackled the sound of thunder once more. He then froze one of the whips and shattered it, then pulling out his two shimmering swords, he pierced them both into his brother's chest. Damion then stumbled backward, while he still held the electric whip. "You put this upon yourself, brother." Kanos walked away slowly as his brother then fell backward over the edge, but doing so, he also wrapped the electric whip around his body, shocking him as he splashed into the icy abyss, never to be seen again.

Kanos then fell to his knees and began to cry. You could see dozens of bodies floating on the icy waters as the last ship left the ice canyon. Dozens of crashed vehicles burned on ice cliffs, bits of pieces scattered everywhere. The snow quickly covered everything up leaving it now as if nothing ever happened. As the ghosts of the Bonteka Lake swept through the ice canyon, they took every soul that perished that day, taking them back to Bonteka Lake through portals as they shortly came back, continuing to follow Scar to Montorious's castle, for they knew his fate. And if Scar knew the true end to this story, he'd surely, without a doubt, know that all is lost. As the day became dark, people made paper lanterns and put them into the sky to honor the four men that died that day. People walked around helping each other that were wounded and needed attending. Scar quickly ran down below to check on Telina. The two hug.

"Are you all right?" Asked Scar as he checked over her just in case.

"Yes, I'm fine." She smiled. "Oh no!" Telina touched Scar's arm. "Look at you. You're all cut up and bleeding."

"I'm all right." Scar tried to sound tough, but Telina then rushed to the bathroom to grab something.

Adam and Aphemis sat down for a drink together, while Scar's robots walked around washing the deck from blood. Floyd and Kanos were at the back of the ship talking.

"I had to do it." Kanos lowered his head in shame. "What will my father and brother Rolan think of me?"

"They will understand," said Floyd. "He had lost his way and chose the evil path."

"But he was my brother!" yelled Kanos as he formed high winds that shook the ship, but he soon calmed down as he just wept.

"There it is!" yelled a soldier as a man then hit him across the head. *Whack!*

"Quiet, you fool," he whispered. "You want them to know we're here?"

"I think it's too late," said another soldier beside them as he raised his hand up trembling as he pointed near the huge castle. Dozens of different types of flying creatures flew toward the ships. Mandare met them swiftly to battle.

As the ships pushed closer to the castle, you could see that Montorious created the whole area, even the ground, to be stone. Ships hit the side of the cliff as the ramps slammed down soldiers from every ship poured out. All the leaders that Scar had gathered stood by their Armies.

Scar stood in front of all of them and spoke, "Men! This is our time. We've come together to defeat an enemy whose power may seem infinite and unstoppable! But we are here now to take back what is ours and this world." Scar drew his sword. "For *freedom!*"

Everyone drew their swords and varieties of weapons as they all yelled storming up the hill toward a path, passing by Scar as he took one last look at Telina aboard his ship before he, too, ran up the hill to his fate. Iendu climbed up the cliff to join the fight as men shot down arrows upon Scar's Army. "Shields!" yelled Kanos who was way ahead of Scar as everyone put their shields over their heads, while they approached a huge gate as Kanos then froze the huge lock and shattered it as they stormed into the enormous courtyard being greeted by twelve-foot-tall monsters wielding axes. "*Kill them all!*" one yelled as more creatures of different shapes and sizes ran out right after them as well as men. As the fighting began to commence, some threw bombs at people as dozens of arrows from Scar's forces shot back at them, hitting dozens of targets. "This way!" yelled king Typhus as his main men followed him into Montorious's lair. Scar, Kanos, and Rolan fought their way through following as well, constantly slashing and clanging against monsters at every corner. Kanos froze many and set multiple on fire. It seemed like a maze.

Montorious's castle was huge with many big rooms and narrow hallways. The group broke down many doors to find the prisoners, but it seemed it was helpless as they were all sweating from the constant cycle. Typhus cursed as he kicked a door.

"What's that? You hear that?" They all began to hear loud echoing.

"*Help us!*" people cried out further down the hallway.

"We're almost there!" shouted Ramos as he began to cough as he was sweating tremendously due to his weight. He stopped to catch his breath as they all ran passed him. "No, it's okay. I'm fine. I'll catch up. Don't mind me," said Ramos to himself as he leaned against the wall looking both directions to be safe.

He then began running once again before the group was out of sight. They took a right as they broke down a door they assumed the noise was coming from while they walked in. It was a huge room filled with dozens of cages with people and monsters.

"Please help us!" Many people began to stick their hands out the bars.

"Get back!" yelled Kanos as he froze the lock, then shattered it. Kanos then ran to another, then did the same.

"Quickly, we must free them and get them to safety," said Typhus as he looked to see Ramos had finally made his way to them.

Ramos spoke, "Watch yourselves. No telling where Montorious is." Scar looked around the room.

"Hmm. No. I don't think he's even here. Seriously, do you think he'd just let us walk right into his castle without confronting us himself? I don't like this. Something's up," said Scar. Adam and Floyd made their way to where Scar was. "Adam!" yelled Scar as he shook his bloody hand. Adam breathed heavily.

"It's hectic out there. Montorious isn't holding back." One man laughed as he shook is head leaned against the wall.

"Why would he? We are in his way of taking over the entire world."

"Okay, that's the last of them!" said Kanos.

"All right. Here's the plan," said Scar. "King Typhus, Adam, Rolan, Kanos, you come with me."

"Don't forget me!" blurted out Floyd. "I'm pretty sure I'd come in handy. I was here before and remember a lot and certain areas."

"Why, how could I forget?" Scar covered his face. "But, yes, Floyd too! And, Typhus." Scar looked at him. "Your men should take the freed captives and other beasts back to my ship."

"Agreed!" yelled Typhus. "Men, move!"

"Yes, sir!"

"Protect them at all costs, especially Telina's family." Scar tried to see if someone would speak up, but there were so many people running and pushing terrified. The people panicked as they followed the men to safety. "All right now. We will search this place for"—a chill ran down Scar's back—"Montorious. And his higher henchmen. Be on the lookout. I'm sure he may have nasty and dangerous traps as well as forces lurking these halls." And as the group pressed on, Scar led them farther and farther into the dark hallways watching every corner to be safe. But what Scar didn't know was he was leading them all to their deaths.

CHAPTER 10

Facing Montorious

The battle raged on while the prisoners that were now freed were safely aboard Scar's vessel. Telina ran to her family, finally being reunited. Morning drew near, and Montorious's forces were almost all defeated. Of course, they were not easy to defeat. These foul creatures of the dark were cunning and sinister. With the help of the Hemanda helped tremendously with their physic capabilities, super-speed, and ablity to form energy balls.

"I remember these hallways," whispered Floyd into Scar's ear.

"Lead the way to his chamber," whisperd Scar. The group slowly made their way deeper into the castle. A cold draft suddenly blew through. They could hear the echo of the battle still comencing outside.

"We're almost there. Make a left here." While the last person made his way and turned, his arm brushed up against the wall, setting off a trap. *Click! Boom!*

"What was that!?" yelled Scar. He spun his head around. The path they had just came from was now blocked off.

"He led us into a trap!" shouted Typhus as he tried to strangle Floyd.

Floyd quickly flew into the air in circles to escape the angry king.

"Quiet. You guys are too loud," said Adam.

"No, I didin't. He must have added new things to his castle. I know nothing of this." Floyd flapped his wings and raised his scorpion tail high in defense, ready to pierce Typhus's hand.

"Can we please move on," said Scar growing impatient trying to keep his cool. "And watch your step, we don't want to set off any more traps." The five continued to walk down the dark narrow hallways, which seemed like forever.

"This is madness. We're lost!" said Rolan.

"How will we even—" Before he could finish his sentence, he stepped on a button on the floor. *Swoosh! Swoosh! Swoosh!*

"Look out!" yelled Floyd. Dozens of arrows were coming straight at them. Everyone quickly dropped to the floor.

"That was a close one." Scar rose back to his feet. Suddenly, there was a loud growling sound that echoed the halls, sounding so dark and dreadful.

"What was that?" said Kanos.

"Something you don't want to meet, that's for sure," said Floyd flying up ahead.

"Try not to set of any more traps, brother."

"It wasn't my fault, Kanos. This place is a death trap." Floyd stopped up ahead.

"Floyd, what's wrong?" asked Scar.

"*Shh.*" Floyd gave Scar a gesture. He slowly made his way up to him, peeking his head around the corner. Four monsters were laughing and eating some type of grotesque-shaped food. They talked among themselves.

"Shouldn't we be out there helping?" the creature asked snickering.

"Nah!" said another waving his huge hand in the air. "They have it handled." Smacking his lips, then grasped his huge cup guzzling down some form of liquid that he let run down his disgusting body that was fat. "If they only knew what was coming." All of them laughed, showing their enormous-sized sharp teeth that were yellow.

"Oh, yes, the real fun shall begin soon," said another. The beast then stood up and went over to a table to grab something.

"Hurry, guys, we need to get past quickly," said Scar to his group. He then prepared to make the first attempt across. Sweat trickled down his forehead. He bolted across with Floyd on his shoulder. Typhus was the next to run across, then the rest. Only one remained. He peeked his head, while the monsters were still eating like pigs as if they hadn't eaten in days. Rolan was ready. He began to run across, but his leg cramped up at the moment. "*Ah!*" He grasped his leg, then looked at the four monsters. They all had stopped eating and were staring at him.

"Get him!" one shouted. They all arose out their chairs, flipping them backward, taking out their weapons. Rolan then quickly froze the entrance of the doorway. He quickly got to his feet and rushed to his group. They ran down the hall. You could hear the frustration in their voices. They pounded hard incessantly against the ice wall. Almost breaking through.

"Run faster. They're almost through!" yelled Rolan. *Boom!* Huge ice chunks flew in the air scattering everywhere. The creatures stormed down the hallway.

"We're coming for you!" Everyone in Scar's group was exhausted, sweating, trying to escape the persistent threat.

"Stop!" yelled Kanos. His eyes began to glow, creating two ice balls in both hands. "Where are they?" Everyone breathed heavily, catching their breath, leaning against the wall.

"I don't know, but let's—" Before Scar could finish, the floor beneath them began to break apart, leading to another part of the castle. Everyone began to run again.

"Damn I'm getting tired of this," said Rolan, running. Unfortunately, he was the first to fall in and landed on his knee. The floor then stopped crumbling.

"Brother!" Kanos turned back after him. He hopped down. "How bad is it? Is anything broken?" He saw his brother holding his knee and reached to touch it. Rolan yelled in agony, grabbing his brother's wrist.

"No. No. It's just badly bruised. I'm fine." Rolan then tried to get up on his own.

"Come on. Let me help you." Kanos helped him up and put his brother's arm over his shoulder.

"I found them!" yelled one of the beast. The two brothers could see a large figure coming straight for them from behind and in front of them.

"Hurry!" yelled Adam leaning over the edge of the broken floor that was starting to reform itself.

Kanos quickly used his powers and picked him and his brother up on currents of wind. Creatures were now almost upon them, stomping, yeilding swords and axes, charging from both sides. The two made it safely back to their friends just in time. There was a loud noise. The floor now sealed completely shut. Monsters cursed below. Scar ran over to his friends.

"Is he okay?"

"No, his knee—"

Before Kanos could finish, Rolan yelled out loud, "Im fine!" Trying to stand on his two feet alone, he stumbled against the wall.

"He needs to get back to the ship!" Typhus reached into one of his pockets and wrapped a piece of cloth around his knee. The loud growling they heard once before erupted again, echoing the hallway.

"He's coming." Floyd flew ahead. "Hurry!" Everyone rushed down the hall to follow Floyd. Kanos was lagging behind with Rolan, trying to keep up the best they could, making turns down hallways. The growls seemed to be getting closer.

"Stop! Leave me, brother. I'll hold whatever it is off."

"No!" yelled Kanos trying to stay strong, still carrying his brother along. The unknown beast was almost upon them. You could smell his foul breath that smelled of spoiled milk and his distinctive repugnant body odor.

"Brother, have reason. Look at me. I'm done for." Floyd flew back to where the two brothers were, then turned to see two big eerie eyes staring back at him and enourmous spiked horn in the shadows.

"It's Yambada! One of Montorious's elite creations. Like the one I fought in Baltar." Kanos lowered his head. His face becoming to look worried.

"Kanos," said Rolan. His brother slowly lifted his head back up looking into his brother's eyes. "Let me go tell father I love him." Kanos tried not to tear up as he let his brother down against the wall.

"Rolan, there's something I must tell you." A loud roar erupted, and the beast was almost to them. It grinned, watching them as if he loved the last moment of helplessness he saw in their eyes. "Go ahead, guys! I'll catch up," shouted Kanos. The group ran ahead.

"What is it? You pick the greatest time to tell me such imperative things, little brother," said Rolan grinning.

"I ran into our brother Damion when we were in the ice canyon. He led Montorious's forces to us. We fought. I...I—" Kanos couldn't get his words out. Rolan's eyes grew in sadness.

"You did what you must. Damion lost his way, blinded by power like some of our other kin." Rolan laid a hand on Kanos's shoulder. "Now go, brother. Some of our kin didn't choose the enemy's side. They must be imprisoned in here still. *Go!*" Kanos stood up and ran off to catch up with his friends, not looking back.

Rolan pulled out his two swords and used one to stand up. "Where are you?" a huge foot stomped out of the darkness, growling, wielding a weapon that had a huge claw at the top of it. On the other hand, it held a giant staff, aiming it toward Rolan and shot it at his chest. He yelled as he collasped to the ground. Kanos could hear the cry of his brother echo the hall. He looked down, knowing what happened. They reached a door finally.

"Here it is," whispered Floyd.

"Okay. Get ready, men." Everyone drew their weapons. Kanos placed his hand on the door. It began to freeze up. *Wham!* He shattered it into tiny pieces. Everyone rushed inside, entering a huge room with statues of some type of symbol and a hallway that led to his bed. "Search the room. Watch your back," said Scar. They all split up. The room felt dark and cold, like death was near.

"Scar, there's nothing here!" yelled Typhus. Everyone then ran back where they came in.

Scar threw over a table. "Where is he?" Lifting his head in the air, then shifting his eyes around the room. "You run away and choose not to fight! Your Army is defeated! You've lost," said Scar breathing heavily. Kanos laid a hand on his friend's shoulder.

"Hey, take it easy, will you?" At that moment, a loud horn errupted.

"What's that? Is it our forces outside? Have they won?" asked Adam.

"*No.*" Everyone turned to look at Floyd. "He's here."

They heard the loud horn again. Everyone ran toward where it was coming from outside on a huge patio. High winds blew. They saw a man with a hood way across the ice. Behind him in the distance were mountains. No one said a word, only watched in horror at what they saw next. Thousands upon thousands gathered behind and beside him. All their hearts felt like they had jumped out their chests. "My goodness," said Typhus, who stepped closer to take a better look. The sky began to be blanketed by flying creatures of all sorts.

If you were a bird in the sky flying over, you could see his infinite Army stretch for miles. More monsters and men ran to join them in the final cause. "He toyed with us! He wanted us to believe it was over." Adam then stepped closer to the edge of the balcony. "We only have three hundred thousand men left. Who knows how many we've lost just by trying to breach inside the front gates. It looks like he has more than that. Two million. Two million!" said Adam, who backed up against the wall and slid down and sat. "All is lost." None of them said a word, while the mysterious person just stood there on the chilled ice, waiting for something. Scar lowered his head thinking, *No.* Everyone turned their head to face Kanos.

"We've come too far to give up now. My brother died believing that. I have more brothers imprisoned here who I can convince to help. I'm going to find them." Kanos then walked off the patio.

"Wait," said Adam, who arose to his feet. "I'm coming." Kanos nodded and smiled.

"As will I." Typhus walked to them.

All but Scar who was leaned over the railing of the balcanoy, then turned his head around to look at them. He took a deep breath then exhaled. "Well, what are we waiting for?"

They all ran off the patio in search for Kanos's brothers. Floyd led the way. You could hear the echoes of men yelling through the halls killing monsters. They turned another corner, runing into Nabeth.

"Scar!" He shook his friend's hand.

"My friend, give word to the rest. Watch yourself in here. There's traps, and there's an Army just behind the castle." Nabeth just grinned.

"I knew that wasn't all he had in store. We will meet them into battle now," said Nabeth sternfully. "Let's move!" Hundreds of Bosari hounds ran past, and men trickled behind.

"Okay, guys, let's check in here." Scar slowly opened the door but was swatted hard by something.

"You all will die!" Raising its huge hammer to crush Scar's skull. Floyd swooped in and pierced the monster in his eye with his scorpion tail. He roared in anger.

Typhus and Adam sneaked up slicing its legs. The beast swung his three-forked tail around stabbing Adam in his arm. Then used his staff and shot something toward Typhus's feet. Kanos jumped in the air yelling, pulling out his two swords and cut his stomach. *Wham!* The creature swatted him off. He cursed while he pulled out the two sharp blades that dripped yellow-greenish blood.

"You will die first for that by your own weapons." He grinned evilly. Stomping toward him, he tossed one so he could have a grip on his staff better. Kanos was a little disoriented. He opened and closed his eyes, constantly gazing upon Adam, who was holding his arm, then Typhus, who was stuck in some type of black muck. Scar rose to his feet.

"*No.* No more friends shall die today!"

He charged the monster dodging the muck that the sinsister beast shot from his staff. Scar pulled out a sword and clanged it with his. The creature kicked him then swung his giant spiked horn around. He ducked. Kanos fianlly regained conciousness and formed two ice spears, ran up, and hopped onto its back, stabbing them into his neck. The monster roared in agony, shaking, falling to his knees.

Kanos ran over to help free Typhus from the muck, creating fire in both his hands an aimed it near the muck. It bubbled, then hardened rapidly, then tore off a piece of cloth from his clothes and wrapped it around Adam's arm.

"Tell me where the two brothers are being held that have powers!" yelled Scar who put a gun to its head. The monster just laughed and coughed up blood.

"I found them!" yelled Floyd, flapping his wings, waiting outside the door for everyone to follow him.

Scar briefly looked back down at the monster who had died, drowned in his own blood. Everyone ran out the room following Floyd down the hall into a huge room where there were many cages. Everyone was in awe once they came to where Kanos's brothers were being held. The cages they were in had their arms and legs in restraints that seemed to suppress them from using their powers.

The worst part was they stood on a platform. Kanos feared whatever awaited below would be deadly. "How are we going to get them out?" asked Kanos growing worried. He then formed wind in both his hands and flew up to his brothers. "Aaron! Sabastain!" Kanos's face lit up. "Hang on. We're going to get you out!"

"Well, hurry!" yelled Sabastain. Kanos then flew back down to the others.

"Okay, we need to search the area. Find anything that could help get them out."

"But how will we know what we find would help and not?" Adam stopped himself from saying something stupid.

"Well, let's get searching!" said Typhus.

"There's some controls over here!" yelled Floyd, who was flying in circles over a huge machine of some sort. Everyone ran over to him. Many buttons flashed different colors, some being a variety of different shapes as well. Scar cursed.

"Which one?" he balled his hand into a fist and slammed it down onto a button on accident. A loud noise then suddenly occurred.

The door of both the door cells slid open.

"You've done it, Scar!" said Kanos.

"Why, um, yes, I did." Scar scratched his head.

"Come on, Scar, just one more button, and they'll be free!"

"Be quiet! I can't concentrate." Scar began to sweat knowing the weight of his friend's brothers lied in his hands. His eyes shifted toward a purple button. "Oh, I hope this works." Another loud noise occurred. A woman operating system then came on. "*System now initiated!*" Scar cursed again, then looked up at the two brothers to see that they were still fine. Shortly after, the two brothers were shouting. Kanos rushed back up to his kin.

"What is it?" He saw nothing. The platforms were still intact, then he looked over the side. "Scar, what have you done?" Everyone below began to be worried as well.

"What did I do?"

"You somehow let loose dozens of creatures at the bottom of this hole!"

"Sounds like Nikato's," said Floyd.

"That's not good. I'll try another!"

"Careful," said Kanos who took another look at the huge beats that were thrashing in the icy waters below. "Scar, I must go and regroup with my men and lead them in the final battle," said Typhus sternfully.

"Okay!" Scar turned to his friend and nodded his head. Adam then rushed over to Scar.

"Let's try this one!" He pressed a dark-orange button.

"No, change it back!" yelled Kanos, for the platform beneath his brothers was slowly being removed from their feet that now dangled in the restraints. Both brothers looked down, knowing they shouldn't have, gazing upon their hideous fate. Adam pressed the same button once more, repeatedly panicking. But it seemed to have no effect in retracting the platform back.

"We're going to die!" yelled Aaron.

"No," said Kanos whose face began to change.

His eyes turned an unusual color. He then portrayed out ice and fire from both his hands that became a swirl, aiming both his hands seperately at both his kin's locks. The immense energy just deflected off once it tried to penetrate the locks. Kanos became angry.

Sweat trickled down Scar's face his eyes scanned over the entire machine, blocking out all the commotion. "I hope this works." *Wham!* He pressed a blue button. Kanos's eyes grew big as he saw that it did not work but instead released his brothers from their restraints. They began to fall. Kanos's eyes turned stormy gray. He yelled loud creating giant hands out of wind and lashed them out to catch his brothers just before they hit the bottom, becoming a treat. He yanked them back up, and they hit the floor hard. The three were now breathing heavily, looking up at each other, smiling. It had been the first time in years they'd seen Kanos.

"Thank you, Kanos, for coming to our aid. We're both ashamed we chose—" Sabastain lowered his head in sadness. Kanos stood up and let out his hands for both his brothers to get up.

"From the looks of how badly you two look, you've atoned for your ways. Now I'd love for us to catch up, but we must take the fight to you know who. Show him what happens when you mess with family." The two brothers that were still on the ground exchanged looks and smiled, nodded, then stood up. The three then gathered to where Scar and the rest were.

"Thanks for assiting in our freedom," Aaron said while shaking Scars hand.

"Well, I couldn't leave you here to be tortured."

"Sorry to break up this divine family reunion, but can we get out of here now!" said Adam, who was already rushing to the exit from which they came. Scar smirked.

"Lets go!"

Everyone else made there way to the door. Floyd flew ahead of everyone leading the way once again down the long hallway. He took them to a walkway to left that led them down a huge fleet of spiral stairs. The five ran down the stairs as fast as they could, which seemed to be endless. Everyone was panting, taking deep breaths.

"This is going to take forever! Brothers!" said Kanos as they stopped walking.

"What is it?" one asked.

"We'll have to use our powers to make the rest of the way faster." The two agreed.

The three brother's eyes all turned green as they began to hover off the ground on currents of wind and floated into the middle of the huge room that looked like a black hole at the bottom. They then channeled their powers and picked up Scar and Adam.

"Whoa," said Scar, joining them in a huddle, slowly floating down to the bottom. Floyd perched himself onto his friend's shoulder.

"We're going to make it," said Adam happily. At that moment, they all heard loud roaring and men yelling.

"Kill them all!" someone shouted. Numerous hostiles appeared all around them in the columns when they continued to float down. They all had bows and arrows and were about to aim straight at them. Kanos just smirked. "Oh, shoot, what do we do now?" said Floyd. Kanos and his brothers quickly began to rapidly form a huge ice sphere around the entire group. Then giant ice spears began to form around the entire sphere and probe out in all directions killing multiple men and beasts. They cried out in agony. Some fell over the side tumbling down. Another brother put his hands on the ice sphere and spontaneously combusted fire out his hands portraying it far enough to burn their enemies.

Scar pulled out his device and pressed a button, then scanned it over his body. He was now covered in complete body armor. "Almost there!" Kanos could now see the bottom of the stairs. "Just a few more feet!" said Kanos.

"Look out!" yelled Sabastain. A huge fireball came straight at them from a Kadaki. It shattered the iceball and the six went tumbling down, hitting the ground shortly after. Everyone groaned and slowly got back up.

"Everyone all right?" asked Scar.

"Luckily, we were already close to the ground." Sabasatin raised his head up to look how high the stairs went, then he heard loud mass yelling. His eyes turned to the stairs. Monsters were storming down the stairs.

"Let's move!" said Floyd, who flew ahead. There was a door. "After we get through, we have to go through the hallway and off the patio should be where your troops are, Scar."

"Okay, you guys go without me!" Everyone stopped running and turned around to look at Scar.

"What? Why?"

"Are you crazy?" said multiple of his friends.

"I'll hold them off. If we don't take care of them now, they'll be right behind our Army before the war even begins. *Go. Now!*" Kanos gave him a look. He didn't want to leave.

"Stay strong, Scar." He then ran up ahead with his brothers with Floyd.

"Don't do this, my friend," said Adam. The creatures were getting closer now, each of them making different terrifying noises. Scar turned his back to Adam to face horde of abominations that were charging straight for him. Some humans were in the ranks as well yelling barbarically.

"It must be done." He pulled out one sword and took two steps forward.

"If this is about what Aphemis had said, then—"

"No. No." Scar turned his head back to his friend. "This is my turn now to be the hero, and you live another day."

Scar partly smiled, then yelled taking on about forty contacts alone. Adam was already gone to catch up with the group. Kanos was almost outside. Adam could see the snow fall. His heart felt empty, thinking the worst, for now he was the one running, and his friend was fighting for his life alone. Scar shot down multiple beasts and men holding his sword in one hand. He then holstered his weapon, pulled out his second sword, and was just about to slice the head off a monster that had tentacles all over its body and arrow-shaped points at the end of all of them. A loud voice yelled, "*S-t-o-p!*" The voice sounded so dark and evil, it made Scar want to throw down his weapons. A chill ran down his back. The remaining monsters and men made way for someone to approach. He then heard evil laughing echo in the air like whoever was watching was everywhere at once.

"Montorious," Scar mumbled.

"You think you've won, boy?"

"Oh, if you only knew." Loud laughter erupted from his enemy's forces.

"Show yourself!" He said, raising his two swords in the air.

"You have heart, boy. But do you really think that's merely enough to defeat me? *I am Montorious!*" The whole room seemed to be shaking. Scar held his ground, while some monsters lost their footing and fell.

"Then why are you afraid to face me like a man?"

All of Montorious's forces eyes grew big in horror that he'd made a grave mistake. Loud footsteps began to approach Scar. The sound was so powerful, it felt like a cannon was going off every time the footsteps got closer. All of the enemy's forces began to kneel, while the man that Scar had heard so much about was almost to him. He was ready.

He could now see him, coming forth with prestige, having a huge abnormal body mass. He had broad shoulders and chest that puffed out. He stood seven feet tall. Covered in body armor, dozens of swords were upon his back all different and other terrible-looking devices strapped to the side of his legs. Eyes that glowed bright gold. Grinning wide as he stood twelve feet from Scar. Scar took the first move and charged his enemy head on. While his opponent just smiled and stayed stationary. Scar was now upon him! *Clang!* At the last moment, he drew his biggest sword like it was light as a feather. Then used his other giant hand to grasp Scar's throat.

"You're such a fool, boy. Predictable." He then stomped over to the door where his friends went and stood outside on his huge patio, raising Scar's body high in the air. "*This is your hero!*" he shouted. Scar's forces just below raised their heads up to see who it was. Montorious then tossed him off the patio far from the castle onto the ice, slamming upon it hard and slid a few feet, then stopped. Not moving a muscle, Montorious then got upon a flying creature to carry him off to his army, while the rest gathered upon a flying vehicle and followed behind. Everyone was shocked at what had just occurred that no one took a shot at taking him out while he flew over them to the other side. Scar still wasn't moving. While he laid there probably dead, Montorious was geting ready to attack to unleash his full might. The snow was still falling. All his friends prepared for the worst knowing they were drastically outnumbered. There was no turning back, for the war to come was finally here.

CHAPTER 11

The War

The two Armies stood, still waiting for someone to make the first move. Thousands of Mandare took to the skies to fight the leigon of hideous flying mutations that awaited. Bosari hounds bared their teeth and howled. Iendu roared majestically. King Typhus then stepped forward and turned to face all the Armies. "Men! Today is a sad day, also a glorious one. Yes, we lost Scar today, the one who brought us together. He helped me find my way back as I'm sure he did for many of you." Scar's closests friends lowered their heads for a moment in sadness. "Today, we fight and will defeat this tyrant!" Soldiers began to cheer. "We will win and bring peace to all the galaxies of this world!" And so Typhus drew his sword. "*For Scar!*" Everyone else yelled "for Scar" following behind the brave king who led the attack, charging in the snow thousands of feet from them, storming toward the enemy as snow splashed up in to the air. Approaching closer to the mad titan and his infinite Army.

He grinned wide. His eyes began to glow gold. "So they choose to fight. Kill them all. I grow tired of these insects disrupting my plans." He then raised his hand high in the air and balled it into a fist making a pose, then let out his hand flat right out in front of him. That gave the signal. Thousands of loyal men and monsters stormed past him shaking the ice ground beneath them. Kadaki fire spitters, Giant crabs, and many more varieties of horrifying creations. Almost to the other side, pulling out their weapons. Air donos and other flying beasts clashed with Mandare. The fighting finally had begun. Shields collided with swords, monsters swung weapons around that had a long chain, and a huge spike ball at the end swinging it, killing many. Men shot hundreds of arrows into the air landing into enemy soldier's necks, eyes, and other body parts. Such a gruesome sight to bear witness to. Bosari hounds shot out quils from their backs, stunning their foes and ripping them to pieces seconds later. Lord Typhus had just sliced a monster in half.

He briefly looked up at the sky. Giant fireballs from Kadaki were coming straight for him and the men beside him. Until Mandare that were on the ground force took action. They jumped into the air forming bluish-green orbs in their hands that they shot at the fireballs as soon as they came into contacts a big explosion occurred. Auroa rained down slowly. They were safe from this imminent danger. Kanos burned creatures every step he took, while another created ice spears, and someone else created wind pushing them into their targets. Sepada quickly tried to create two massive ice tornadoes out of the snow. Four dozen soldiers charged him. He yelled while the two ice tornadoes were in his hands as he thrust them toward them just in time. Whisking them into the air. Spikes were them formed inside the two white tornadoes cutting up the monsters and men inside. They cried for mercy, but none was given.

"They just keep coming!" yelled Adam, who was now back to back with Kanos. Kanos then looked afar to the mountains where he could see many figures still coming to the battle. "Look out, Kanos!" Adam stabbed a man in the back just before he was about to kill him. He looked down at the man who began to pour out blood. Then looked back up.

"Close call." Kanos grinned.

He then formed two ice spears, then aimed for this weird beast. The spears just broke in two once they touched their spiked shoulders. "Oh boy." The beast roared then charged him head on squishing men every step.

"Whoa," said Adam, who stood beside him.

"Stay back. I got this. It looks like your hands are full anyway." Adam spun around. A Barzo and a Kadaki were charging him also. He sighed. Going back to back with his friend once more.

"Good luck to you!" They both then charged their enemies. Battling it out to the death. Kanos clanged his two shimmering swords with the monster who had two giant swords for hands. The two headed thing snarled. Kanos also spotted that it bore the insignia of a giant M on its shoulder. "You must be one of the elite! I've killed your special forces before." Kanos smirked, becoming overconfident. The creature then whipped its tail around. This wasn't an ordinary tail. Something then clamped onto Kanos's shoulder armor sinking in giant teeth! He looked an it was a giant snake! The monster had a snake for a tail. Kanos yelled in agony. The creature then laughed and said something in another language. Kanos was still fighting holding both his swords, pushing them against the beast swords. Both trying to get the upper hand. "How are you doing over there?" Kanos glanced over to see he killed the Kadaki. Covered in many bullet holes. Still going toe to toe with the other one. *Wham!* The creature kicked Kanos in the gut. He slid across the ice over to Adam. Who'd just stabbed the beast in the knee. It roared infuriated.

"Are you okay, Kanos?" he quickly helped him up.

"I'm fine, just lost my footing. That's all." The creature that Kanos was fighting slowly came forward. Something odd then happened. One of the heads could move itself all around the body. Kanos cursed. "Give me a break." The two friends went back to fighting. While snow began to pour down harder. The fighting never stopped, not even for a moment. Hours had gone by. It seemed that Scar's forces hadn't even broken through Montorious's first wave yet. Still, they fought valiantly and courageously.

Why, you could hear the war rage for miles away. It was so loud with so much death. That's when the ghosts of the Bonteka Lake poured out of their many portals appearing in different spots on the battlefield engulfing it. Sucking the souls out of the dead. The two Armies continued fighting like nothing was happening, even though they could see them. Many left taking the souls back where they belonged. While this was being conducted. The ghost that bothered Scar was searching for him. He shimmered in and out of the snow. Finally, he spotted him. He grinned wide flying over to him slowly with the black cloak over his ghastly face. Floyd flew over the battlefield dodging monsters that were fighting each other. Many enemy beasts recognized him, leaving him be. He continued trying to find his friend. His eyes raced back and forth below.

"Found him!" he then turned his eyes to see a black figure going to Scar. "*No!*" Floyd dived down out of the sky quickly to his friend. "Scar! Wake up!" Pleading, but there was no response. "I know you're still alive! You got to be. We need you!" He tugged upon his hair with his beak.

Floyd began to fear the worst had happened. But he had one more solution. He took off high into the air leading away from the battle, flying over the castle back to Scar's ship. Flying past people, he yelled for Telina. Shifting his three eyes from left to right, then flew down below deck. It was very crowded. Many people were trying to find rooms. Finally spotting Telina directing people to available rooms. Floyd flew over to her, while someone tried to swat him down.

"It's his bird!" one shouted.

"They've found us!" a woman cried out.

"Why haven't we left yet?" one demanded.

"Everyone please calm yourself," said Telina.

"*Quiet!*" yelled a voice that stepped next to her. Making everyone become silent.

"Thank you, Father."

"Telina," said Floyd flapping his wings out of breath. She laid out her arm for him to rest upon it.

"What is it, Floyd?" her face growing worried.

"It's Scar" he looked down a moment. She covered one hand over her mouth. "Montorious had him by the neck, and...and"— Floyd paused—"he threw him far upon the ice, and he isn't moving. But I know he's still alive. I can't wake him."

"Don't trust that bird!" yelled a man.

"He's lying, just wants to take us back to Montorious!" someone then tried to grab him, but he pierced their hand with his scorpion tail. The man cursed holding his hand like a wounded animal.

Telina then stood up on a stool and shouted, "Everyone, calm yourselves! He's on our side. So leave him alone!"

Everyone then dispersed muttering things to each other going to their rooms. Telina then rushed to her room to grab something and put it in a bag. "Take me to him." Following behind Floyd almost to the stairs that led to the top deck till her father stopped her.

"What are you doing? You're not going out there!"

"Father, stop." She turned to face him.

"No, you listen. It's too dangerous out there!"

"Father, I have to. The man I love is out there." The man then made a livid expression toward his daughter.

"Love? What is this!" Someone then opened a door to one of the rooms.

"Is everything all right?"

"Yes, mother."

A little girl then peeped her head out the room holding onto the woman's pants leg. Telina then pressed forward again.

"*No!*"

"*Stop!*" shouted her father.

"Jack! Calm down," said the woman standing outside the door, holding her younger daughter now in her arms.

"No. I refuse to lose another child!" Telina then sighed.

"Dad, Jasper isn't dead."

"No. But he might as well be. I disown him! From what's he's become!" Everyone then gave him a look, like he'd just said something he'll regret.

"Jack?" said his wife. His face was red. He took one last look at his daughter, then stormed into the room she was in. Telina then just looked at her mother. "Go! Your friend doesn't have much time left."

"Yes, she is right!" said Floyd. Telina then rushed off with Floyd pulling the hood overhead, and she used the scarf to cover her mouth. She rushed off the ramp, trying to take as big steps she could in the steep snow that led to the huge castle.

The wind blew strong. It stung her face a bit. Floyd constantly flapped his wings harder to get the snow off. She finally made it to the top, standing there in awe for a moment. Sadness grew in her eyes. So many dead bodies around her. Fires were still in some places slowly dying out. Mandare piled over top of mutated beasts. Creatures and men lay everywhere. Telina slowly walked past the endless sight of corpses. Looking upon some people she knew from Baltar. Beginning to tear up.

"Why is there so much evil in this world? What can we do against such malevolent hate?" She then knelt down to look at a man's face she recognized. It was Ramos. Floyd perched himself on her shoulder.

"Sometimes life can be so cruel and unfair. Making it so that we believe we can't go on, but we must for evil like this prospers when we do nothing. Ramos believed that, and he died believing that." Floyd then looked down in sadness. he remembered meeting him. Telina then wiped her face from tears, then stood up.

"Okay. Let's go save Scar." Floyd flew back into the cold wispy sky that blew snow sideways. Both now making their way into the castle.

"This is the safest route," said Floyd. Flying passing many rooms, she ran fast trying to keep up. The further they got, they began to hear a man shouting for help.

"What, or who was that?" asked Telina. She began to grow frightened.

"No one important." Floyd looked back at her, then straight again. Continuing their way past many doors. They then took a right. They then were coming up to the door where the shouting was coming from.

"*Hey*! Who's there?" The unknown person could hear footsteps of someone approaching and a loud fluttering sound. Telina glanced into the room passing by. "Wait!" he yelled.

Telina then stopped ten feet past the door to catch her breath. Bending down breathing heavily with her hands on her knees. She then stood back up and turned her head around to hear the man was still shouting. She then turned around fully back to where he was and entered the room.

"Telina! We don't have time for this! Scar needs us!" yelled Floyd. She looked upon a man that had his legs chained, and his hands suppressed in locks. His back was to the wall, his entire body covered in some type of muck.

"Who is this man?" She gave him a mean look.

"A friend of Scar's, I can assure you." Floyd then flew into the room. Once he saw who it was, his face lit up, then his eyes raced the room to find something that'd help free him. He spotted a long table in the corner with a bunch of stuff on it. Floyd then flew over to where the two were and dropped a key into her hands.

"Hurry. Free him!"

"Wait. What? I don't know him. This could be some type of trap." She then turned around to leave the room.

"Wait!" the man pleaded. "You need to help Scar, right?" She stopped walking her, back still turned from him.

She slightly then turned her head back a little and said, "Yes, he's wounded upon the ice by Montorious." The man's eyes grew big, then looked down in sadness.

"I can help him. You just have to set me free." She studied him for a moment, then twirling the key in her hands. She first undid the locks on his legs, then went to his hands. The man rubbed his wrists.

"Okay, so now what do we do to get you out out this muck?" asked Telina confused. He then smiled.

"Well, now it's my turn." He raised his hands angling them two feet from his body.

His eyes became the color of molten lava, then began to portray it out his hands onto the muck. Shortly after, he quickly portrayed out ice that froze it hard. He balled up his hands into fists and smashed free. The man then tried to stand up but fell back down. Telina quickly saw the issue and rushed around the room to find things that could help. She broke legs off a chair, then found some rope and tied them together, then she broke the doorknob off the door and put it on top of the wooden staff she made and helped the man up and gave it to him.

"Name's Rolan. You must be Scar's female friend." She blushed slightly.

"Can we please move along? He won't be anyone's friend if we don't hurry!"

"Yes! You two go on. I have to go back to the ship. I'll try to convince some of the men we freed to help us fight."

"They aren't going to help. Some just wish we were dead anyway." Rolan just stared at her confused. Floyd looked at her knowing. Floyd then told him, which way to get out. The three went their separate ways. Telina continued to follow Floyd while in deep thought.

Wondering if they'd make it to him in time. It felt like an endless maze to her the fortress of the evil being who terrorized so many. A beast himself. Snow continued to fall while Scar still lay upon the chilling ice, not having much time left. The ghost of the Bonteka Lake just waited, for he knew he'd be his in a matter of time. Rolan moved as fast as he could with the crutch. Edging now to the entrance of the castle stepping into the graveyard. Passing bodies. Limping making his way to the hill. Rolan tried to step carefully but slipped and tumbled down the bottom. The cold wind blew through his hair, struggling to get up. He could hear music playing and a bright bonfire on his friend's ship. He slowly dug his hand in the snow in anger, then reached for the wooden staff and stood up and made his way across the ramp. He drew closer to the noise. He saw many men eating, drinking, and laughing having a wild time. Some were being a little intimate with women out in the open. *Whoosh!*

A huge ice beam was aimed at the fire putting it out instantly. The music stopped. Everyone looked Rolan's way. "You should be ashamed of yourselves! Too coward enough to fight. As you stay out here." He paused and looked down at a women and a man. "Having fun while thousands of men and creatures alike are dying! Right now for freedom so this evil will not spread everywhere else! Can't you hear the cries out there?" He then pointed toward the castle. "You were able to see smoke and glimpses of aerial battle behind the fortress."

"It's pointless!" yelled a man. "They're outnumbered. There's too many." Rolan then created whirls of wind in both his hands raged in anger.

"Wars are not won by mere numbers! It's from strategy and strength in each other!" Everyone on the deck fell over plates of food, flipped over chairs, and wisped over the edge of the ship. Rolan calmed himself breathing heavily. "I came here hoping to find men who were ready to make a hard decision but choose the right one. Instead, I just see animals. Cowards. Selfish men. Have you forgotten who was it that came to save you from that wretched place you were imprisoned in? It was Scar! Adam! My brother! And myself!" Rolan's eyes turned crystal blue, then fiery red. "I should kill you all where you stand." Intense fire began to portray out both his hands. Ready to wipe them out. But then slowly retracted the flames back into his hands. "No, I'll let you stay out here while we fight, and if we all die, at least we died for something." Rolan then turned to go back the way he came limping. Till a woman stopped him that came from below deck.

"Well, you aren't going to be doing much if your leg is all beaten up. Look at you. Sit down. I have some things that will help." Rolan didn't argue. He sat. She rubbed some medicine over his wound. He yelled in pain. "Here. Also drink this."

"Thank you." The lady smiled.

"No, thank you for what you're doing." Rolan then looked at his knee to see whatever she used healed his wound quickly. He was able to move about without the staff. He then stood up and nodded to the woman and smiled, then made his way to the ramp.

"Wait!" Rolan spun around with an ice ball formed in one hand. A man with a scruffy beard came up to him reaching out his hand.

"We will help you fight." Rolan then made the ice ball disappear and shook the man's hand. He then looked behind him to see people had gathered spare weapons and were coming to where they were.

"Let's move then!" He turned around then started running off the ramp up the hill.

"You heard him!" said the man with the beard. Everyone then ran following behind. Three thousand men strong heading to the war. They ran up the hill, all barbaric yelling. Approaching the courtyard, many stopped to pick up fallen soldiers' weapons. Then stormed Montorous's castle. Telina could now see the patio from afar.

She then stopped to catch her breath once more. Bending down resting her hands on her knees.

"Are you all right?" asked Floyd.

She looked up and said, "Yes."

Continuing to make their way almost to the patio until all sudden a man came out a door blocking the entrance.

She froze. Floyd then went into defense mode blocking him from her. Ready to pierce him with his scorpion tail. The unknown man wore body armor, two swords were on his back, and a dagger on his left leg. He then took off his helmet and stared at them.

"Telina?" he asked. She then took off her hood.

"Jasper." She took a step back. He then smiled.

"Why, that's no way to treat family." He took a few steps forward.

"Stay back!" yelled Floyd squinting his three eyes at the man. Jasper snapped a look of hate toward the bird and focused his attention now on him. He pulled the dagger from the pocket on his leg and drew it on him.

"How dare you even show your face! Traitor!"

"I knew I couldn't be a part of his plans any longer!" said Floyd. Twitching his scorpion tail.

"Stop it!" yelled Telina. But the two paid no mind to her.

"He created you! He owns you!" Jasper snickered and grinned wide.

"No!" Floyd then swooped closer to him about to pierce him in his neck.

Scout appeared barking and snarling and pounced on Jasper. He dropped his dagger and helmet. "It's okay, Scout." Floyd then flew onto the man's chest and raised his tail high.

"Do it," he said, eagering him on laughing. "Do it!" he yelled. "Floyd." He then looked over at Telina.

"Don't." He could see sadness built up in her eyes. He then looked back down at the smiling man. Then flew off him. Jasper then gave an expression of superiority picking back up his stuff. Then walked closer to Telina now standing beside her. Then he took a deep breath an exhaled.

"Oh, my little sister, where were you off to in such a hurry?" He walked with her to the patio. Telina's heart began to race. "Look at all this. Tell me what do you see." He raised both his hands in the air. Telina's eyes raced back and forth to the sky and down below.

"I see death, brother." Her face grew with sadness. Constant fighting was at work from bullets to swords, magic, and element using. Monsters fell down from the sky. Flying vehicles blew up in the air.

"There he is," whispered Floyd into her ear. She looked and saw a speck far across from the battle that must been Scar.

"No, my sister." Jasper turned to look at her. "I see a new era dawning, a necessary cleansing that must be done." Her brother's eyes glared at the battlefield becoming more evil looking. Loud yelling was then heard behind them echoing the halls. "Ah, so more people came to fight." He put upon his helmet and reached into his pocket pulling out something.

It was a device of some sort. He pressed a button. A huge flying machine then flew from on top of the castle to him. He then boarded it.

"Jasper, don't do this!" His sister grabbed her brother's arm.

"Let go of me!" He nearly almost pushed her to the ground. "I've made my choice. Join us, sister. It's not too late." He held out his hand grinning. Telina then shook her head no taking a few steps back. "Fine. The next time we meet, little sister, it won't be as pleasant." He then started up the machine and took off heading to the war shooting his way through, dodging giant diamond-shaped daggers that were shot from Mandare. Telina then ran down the stairs rushing to where Scar was. Floyd was already there waiting. She knelt down and laid his head upon her lap, then pulled out the bottle containing some type of liquid.

"I hope this works."

She poured the purplish liquid into Scar's mouth to drink. Waiting patiently for a result, but nothing happened. He was so cold. Telina put her hand upon his cheek. His face started to slowly clear up, and body became slightly warm.

"Is he okay?" asked Floyd.

"For now, but he needs to rest awhile and get more warm." Telina then called Scout over to Scar, and he lay over him. "Where's Rolan? Hope he gets here soon." She looked at Floyd upset. "I mean he'll be here in no time!" She smiled then looked at the battling Armies. Then saw a ghost that was approaching from afar. It astro-projected itself through fighting people. Coming closer, it laughed evilly. Now upon them looking down at Scar.

"It's almost time," said the ghost.

He waved his hand, and a portal appeared. Things moved inside. It changed to multiple colors: green, purple, red, and blue. "No, he'll make it," she cried out. Everyone at that moment heard loud mass yelling coming from the patio. The three turned to look. It was Rolan! Some people from both sides looked up. Some cheered while others shouted come and die with the rest of them. Rolan then flew down on currents of wind off the patio. Then ran over to where Scar was. Men up top stormed down both sides of the steps. Charging into battle being met instantly with a foe. Rolan was finally to his friend and angled his hands three feet from his body and began to warm his body.

"That won't work. He's already dead" The ghost snickered reaching down to take his soul.

"No, look!"

You could see his hand start to move, then his legs. Scar made a loud groaning sound. His eyes then began to slowly open. Rolan then stood up and made room for Telina who held him in her arms. "You claim no soul today, vermin," said Rolan. The ghost then shimmered floating his body directly into his face.

"But you're wrong. Oh, I've claimed many souls today." He then pointed to his fellow ghosts who were collecting their prizes. "But him!" He pointed his long black nail at Scar. "That's who I want!"

"Why is he so important to you?" asked Rolan. The ghost then made a loud evil snarl.

"That doesn't concern you." Scar was finally fully conscious. He looked into Telina's eyes and smiled. He was about to say something till she kissed him passionately. They were shortly interrupted by Floyd.

"Hey, now don't forget about me! I helped too."

"What? You want a kiss too?" Scar tried to pick Floyd up, but he hopped away from him.

"Don't you dare." Scar laughed.

"Thank you, friend." He nodded his head. He then brushed Telina's hair behind her ear and then spotted his other friend. "Rolan? You're dead!" Since he saw him talking with one of the dead.

Rolan then looked down at Scar and smiled. "I'm definitely alive." The ghost then floated over to him to his face. His eyes slowly began to turn red. "Rejoice now, Scar, bringer of freedom and courage, for you will be mine one day." Scar then squinted his eyes, then sat up to face the ghost.

"No, I won't." The two just stared at each other for a moment like a gun standoff was in effect. The monster then made a terrifying look upon his face baring his teeth. But Scar showed no fear. The ghost then burst into dark auroa retreating back into the portal. It twirled then disappeared. His friend then helped him up. Scout licked his hand his tail sparked off light.

Scar then walked to the side of the castle and sat down. He prayed his device wasn't too damaged as he reached into his pocket to retrieve it. The screen was cracked, but the buttons were still intact. Scar pressed a button, and numerous holograms shot into the air.

"What are you looking for?" asked Rolan.

"Reinforcements," stated Scar giving his friend a serious look.

Swiping through the holograms and tapped one, then aimed the device near a huge open spot on the ice away from the battle. The device made a loud sound. Suddenly, a light shone, and robots began to appear holding laser guns. Some had other big weapons that shot other things. They lined up. All his friends looked in awe. More robots kept coming until the device stopped shining, and a light on the device became red. "Full capacity released," said a woman recording. Scar explained to them that his device wouldn't be able to give any more until one week passed.

"Well, I think you brought enough!" Rolan smiled gazing upon the robots. "How many?" he asked.

"Fifteen thousand," said Scar with pride. Telina then handed him his helmet.

"You be careful out there, mister." She looked worried then smiled.

"Oh, you know me. I'm always bashing myself through things." He smiled back, grinning. She then punched him in his chest playfully, then hugged him. "I'll see you again." Giving her a look.

"Go back to the ship. I don't want you getting hurt. That goes for you two as well."

He stared at Floyd and Scout briefly. Scout howled as if he understood. Telina then kissed his cheek and held his hand while walking away. Floyd yelled a smart comment back to Scar while he sat upon Scout's back heading back into the castle.

"Try not to die. It's always fun taking your food from you!" Scar just shook his head and laughed, then turned to face the real importance and got serious.

"Rolan, you ready?" The two shook each other's hand roughly.

"I was just waiting on you. You sure you don't want to go back with her?" Rolan teased. Scar just smirked then put upon his helmet.

"Robots! prepare for battle."

All of the robots' eyes then lit up white light. Then turned on their guns. Scar then yelled loud as he could. "*M-o-n-t-o-r-i-o-u-s. I'm coming for you!*" He then began to run straight to the war pulling out his extra two swords. Rolan formed ice spears while he ran and threw them far as he could. His eyes then turned gray as he kept them all in the air controlling them. Both Armies ceased fighting. Loud rumbling shook the ground beneath.

"What is that?" demanded Montorious angrily. When he'd just crushed the life out of a poor Bosari hound.

"My lord," said a giant monster that was cut up all over his body holding in one of his scaley hands a mangled soldier leaving a trail of blood behind him. "It appears that Scar lives."

"Impossible. That boy is stronger than I thought," said Montorious to himself.

"Shall I send for a legion of air dono to eradicate him?" The two then saw Rolan and Scar break through their forces astoundingly quick giving the rest of their side a way through as well.

"*No.*" His eyes then shone gold. "Let *him come. This time, I will rip him into pieces!*" The two then turned around to face forty soldiers that were yelling charging them. Montorious grinned wide raising his hands, pulling off his huge double-sided axe from his back. The creature beside him threw the carcass from his hand, stood on two feet, beat his chest, then ran on all fours to follow his lord into combat. They continued to push through Montorious's Army. People cheered.

"We can defeat them!" shouted Kanos. He stood next to Adam. They both were covered in blood, exhausted from the tiresome assaults. Someone else was coming toward them that they were unaware of, someone who turned to the dark side. Adam had just stabbed a beast through his body, but he was then hit from behind in that split second. He yelled in agony falling to the ground, holding his side. He then could feel himself being raised up off the ground somehow. He couldn't see who it was doing this. Adam was then thrown over to where Kanos was behind him. Kanos had just sliced a beast in half. All his insides poured out onto the cold ice steaming the ground. Guts and other weird-shaped organs lay in a huge pile. His body then fell on both sides to the ground. He then spun around and looked down.

"Adam! Are you all right?" he helped him up.

"I'm fine, just a small cut," said Adam, who held his side. His eyes then shifted from where he was thrown. A tall man wearing black-and-silver armor with a gold symbol in the middle with a giant M in the middle. He slowly stepped closer passing, fighting men and monsters. He took off his battle mask. Kanos's face grew big in awe.

"Zepa," said Kanos. The man smiled evilly.

"Brother, we finally meet again." Kanos then raised his sword high toward his kin.

"Why, brother?" The man just grinned.

"I'm hurt, this is how you treat family? I haven't seen you in ages." Zepa stepped a few feet closer to them.

"I don't want to hurt you, brother," said Kanos. The man laughed.

"Funny, I was about to say the same thing." He reached down and slowly pulled out one sword on his waist. "You sure you want to do this, brother?" he glared his eyes toward Kanos. "It's not too late. You can still join us." He raised his hands high holding a sword in one.

"Never! Look around us, Zepa. Is this what you want? All this destruction, pain, and death." Kanos looked down in pity. "I could never join in such horrible ways."

"Montorious will win! You have no idea what's really happening and coming." He then drew his other sword. The two then lit up becoming electrical charged and ice crystals began to coil around the two swords.

"Are you well enough to fight?" asked Kanos

"Of course. I never felt better! Told you I was fine." He then stepped in front of him to face his friend's brother.

"No." He laid a hand of his friend's shoulder. "This is my fight." His eyes turned grayish black. Adam then nodded his head and stepped back to watch the fight, still being aware of his surroundings, of course.

"So be it, brother. You have no reason in your madness. Montorious has truly made you lost." Kanos's swords lit up a more intense heat than usual. Zepa laughed.

"Oh, brother, you do know I'm the strongest out of all of us?"

"We'll see about that today."

Kanos then charged him yelling. His brother just gave him an evil look, then did the same. They both jumped into the air on currents of wind. Clanging swords together, fire burst immense heat from Kanos's swords, while lighting surged some out of his brother's swords. Both of them slowly came back down to the ground feet first, still fighting insanely, clashing swords incessantly. They used their powers often too. Both brothers were sweating. Then both of them backed up and threw down their swords.

"I'm impressed Kanos." Zepa grinned forming a huge ice ball in his hands. "But let's see how you do against using our true power!"

His eyes turned entirely ocean blue aiming the ball of ice toward him an shot it at his brother. It was almost to him but then suddenly burst into dozens of needles. Kanos then raised his hands and intense fire poured out. *Wham!* His brother had ran into the fire and punched him in the face. Kanos fell to the ground. Adam shouted his friend's name. But Kanos just said he was fine and quickly got back up and began using martial arts against his brother. "No look! Watch out!" pleaded Adam pointing to the sky. Kanos had just jumped into the air and kicked Zepa in the face. *Whoosh!* Intense fire came down from the sky. Three air donos and other multiple creatures swooped down, coming straight for him. Scar continued to slash through many monsters making his way up the mountain where fighting was everywhere up there. Rolan and Scar had gotten separated by all the excitement. Scar breathed heavily. His eyes raced across the ice to find his true opponent. There he was! Fighting multiple men at once. Montorious.

He could see his eyes shine from where he was. Fighting with extreme talent and swiftness. Scar cursed. "I'll never make it to him at this rate." But he then looked to the skies and smiled, waving his hands. While the wind blew strong, snow twirled in circles. A flying Mandare came quick to his aid. "I need you to take me to that man." Scar pointed. The beast made a funny noise. Scar nodded his head understanding and smiled about to hop on. He looked at the Mandares body that was covered in blood and deep cuts and claw marks from fighting. The monster then flew high into the air on his way toward Montorious. Air donos tried to stop their advancement, swooping down, blowing fire. The Mandare dodged it safely, shooting out diamonds from its tail in defense. That missed some the monster's face getting caught in their shells instead. Few of them went tumbling down out of the sky to their demise. Scar saw he was close, so he stood up ready to jump. The Mandare lowered down. Suddenly, another monster roared coming from above, ready to devour Scar completely its mouth opened up wide. He jumped off just in time hitting the ground. He then got up, brushed snow off his body, and put his helmet back on his head. There he was fifteen feet away. Scar slowly made his way to him watching his surroundings.

While he drew closer, he could see that he'd grasped a man by his neck and held him over the mountainside. Dozens of fighting was commencing around them. Scar stopped a safe distance and shouted, "*M-o-n-t-o-r-i-o-u-s!* Leave him be! And face me." The man that was having the life strangled from him tried to pull Montorious's massive hand away. He grinned evilly watching the poor man's face change colors.

"You dare give me orders, boy!"

"Forgive me, Scar. I tried," said that man, coughing. His eyes became teary.

"Your tyranny ends here!" yelled Scar. He laughed evilly again. His eyes then shone slightly brighter.

"No, boy. The world will be mine." He grinned wide. "And everything in it shall follow me." He then looked at Scar with the corner of his eye. "Or *Die!*"

"*No!*" shouted Scar.

Montorious had released the man from his grip, leaving him to rot in the dark abyss below. Scar reached out his hand in despair as if he could have stopped this tragedy. He then turned his focus on to Scar and charged him, making the ground shake with every step. The ground began to crack beneath them, which they weren't aware of. Kanos put his hands into the air yelling. He shot out an ice beam that began to form an ice shield that formed into the shape of a dome that formed around the three. The flying creatures that swept down clashed into it roaring and began slashing it. "*Ha! Ha!* You think that this will stop them?" Zepa spat out blood from his mouth, then picked back up his swords and twirled them.

While his brother lay upon the ice exhausted, the beasts were still breaking through. Some blew fire that rapidly melted it. "Goodbye, brother." Zepa raised both his swords ready to pierce his body. Until the noise outside the dome stopped and then a loud crash was heard, Zepa was hit from behind falling to the ground. Someone then helped up Kanos to his feet. Once he saw who it was, his face lit up. He hugged him tight. He laughed briefly.

"Yes, brother, I am alive." Rolan then looked down at Zepa, who was now beginning to stand back up. "We'll take him on together," said Rolan looking at his brother seriously.

"You both will die!" Zepa's eyes changed to be purple and a white line came in the middle. He then charged them, while the ice beneath them began to crack.

They felt it start to split, but they paid no mind to it. The three began fighting using sword techniques and their incredible powers. Amplifying them more to have the upper hand. All the fighting shook the mountaintop, while snow continued to fall. This war didn't seem to cease. While Montorious and Scar continued to battle it out on the mountaintop along with many others. The skies were still covered in flying monsters, vehicles, and supernatural humans. Nabeth's people were still using their psychic powers to bring flying vehicles tumbling out of the sky crashing onto their own forces. *Clang!* Scar had just hit his nemesis's shoulder armor with his sword. He then ducked shortly after. Montorious tried to slice his throat. "You fight well, boy, but it will not save you." He then wrapped his hands around a huge oversize rock covered in ice that appeared to be in the ground.

He yelled. His veins popped out his neck and on his arms. His eyes shone bright as he ripped it out of the ground leaving a huge equator left. Snow rolled off the huge rock as he held it over his head. Then threw it toward Scar. He dived to the ground quickly before his face was smashed. The huge rock continued to soar through the air till it hit another mountain. *Boom!*

Scar stood back up and turned his head back to see where the large boulder had hit. His eyes suddenly grew wide, for a rush of snow was coming down the mountain where the rock was thrown. He then spun his head back around to see his enemy was walking casually toward him, pulling off a huge double-sided axe from his back glaring at Scar. "*Avalanche!*" yelled a soldier. Everyone stopped fighting for a moment. Many tried to run, but it covered them quickly, making its way toward Scar. There was nowhere to run! The rush of snow came like a rampaging stampede of animals roaring like a lion. The avalanche covered monsters and men, covering the entire battlefield below. If that wasn't bad enough the ice floor finally had enough and became unstable. The ice split in multiple areas. Soldiers and monsters fell between the cracks. Montorious yelled while he swung his double-sided ax. "If we die, then you shall die at my hand!" He and Scar still fought. Some of the ice was created into ice towers where people still fought upon. Some towers leaned, tilting, colliding into other towers. Making both tumble down. The two leaders still fought insanely trying to kill thee other.

Montorious slammed his axe down to crush Scar's skull but missed and hit the ice and got his weapon stuck. He yelled and cursed tugging. Scar now knew this was his chance to take out the horrid evil man. The ice tower split more, and his enemy was able to pull out the axe, but Scar charged him yelling and dived tackling him in his side. Montorious saw where he was about to go he looked at Scar angrily reaching for his side weapon. While he and Scar went tumbling down. Scar still yelled having his sword aimed at Montorious's chest. While snow wisped and blew hard. The supernatural man's eyes shone bright gold more than ever. Pulling out a huge knife. The two continued to fall down the dark abyss with other people and beasts at the same time. While they reached closer to the bottom, Montorious and Scar looked each other in the eyes unfearful of death. What happened next would change the fate of the war and the balance of the world itself.

CHAPTER 12

Genocide

M ontorious and Scar both fell to the bottom hard piercing each other with their weapons, surprisingly surviving the fall. The other bodies of fallen soldiers from both sides broke their fall. While the two leaders were unconscious. Yet another avalanche was coming down the dark abyss. Scar groaned rolling off Montorious, trying to get some distance between them. While the rolling massive snow still was approaching like a stampede of wildebeest. "*No! It will not end this way. Scar, you will die!*" Montorious grabbed Scar's ankle while the huge sword that Scar had pierced his chest inches away from his heart. While Scar had a giant knife in his side. His armor helped prevent it going any further. Blood dripped and rolled off his body. Scar began to kick his enemy in the face. While he turned his head up for a moment to see that many had survived the fall and were fighting once more. Thousands lay dead. Many struggled to get back up. The avalanche was nearly upon them. Scar kicked his face harder, finally breaking free. He crawled as fast as he could. Yelling in agony of the pain in his side. Just in time as tons of snow came crashing. "*No!*" yelled Montorious. He tried to get up. His eyes shone evilly. *Whoosh!* The snow covered him completely. Scar looked back breathing heavily while holding his side looking upon the tons of snow that covered his nemesis. Scar began to smile. But suddenly, a hand burst out of the snow all bloodied up. His hand then began to shake and collapsed back down on the snow. Scar's eyes grew big, for he'd just witnessed the demise of Montorious. Scar continued to lay on the chilled snow holding his side, then slowly began to reach for the giant knife. He cried out in agony while he pulled it out and tossed it. Then looked to the skies to see that the intense aerial battle seemed to be slowly diminishing while Mandare swept down to where Scar was and picked up the wounded. "Scar!" shouted Nabeth.

He fought his way through monsters and men using his superspeed. "Are you all right, my friend?" He leaned down to examine his wound, then glanced over to the huge pile of snow and the giant hand that lay crippled. Scar breathed heavily.

"I… I defeated him. Montorious is dead." Nabeth's eyes grew wide.

"Are you sure?" He then glanced over once more to where the dead leader lay. "Come. Let me get you to safety. Your wound is too severe to fight."

"No! I'm fine."

"Scar," said Nabeth, who then laid a hand upon his shoulder. "You've done enough. Now let us do our part and rid this earth of the remaining evil that lives." He turned his head to look at the what few stragglers that were left still putting up a fight. Then faced Scar once more and smirked. "We've got this covered." A Mandare then swooped down to where they were at. Nabeth then helped Scar up to get upon the beast. "Take him back to his ship." The creature roared then took flight into the sky flying over the battle.

Scar looked down to see the entire area had been destroyed. Ice had broken apart the ground. That led all the way to Montorious castle that still stood. All that was left inside were empty rooms and dead followers of their fallen lord. "Brother!" yelled Rolan. He began to dig snow up with his hands in search to find Kanos. He then laid his hands upon the ice and heated it with hands, making it melt rapidly. Finally reaching his brother who was unconscious. Rolan held him in his arms, his brother slowly began to open his eyes. Slowly lifting up his hand, pointing one finger at something. "Yes, I know,

Kanos. I'm here. Everything is going to be okay now." Kanos began to tremble while still pointing behind his brother. Rolan finally realized what he meant and spun around just as Zepa was three feet away and was yelling, swinging his giant sword. Rolan dived out the way but not before he was cut deeply on his arm. Zepa then put his sword to Kanos's neck. While his arm dripped blood. From the fall, his face didn't look too pretty either. It had cuts all over. One eye was red. His hair was stained in blood. He then raised his sword about to slice the head off his weak brother but stopped.

"I'm not going to kill you yet. I want you to see me kill Rolan first! Watch his eyes lose life and that deep pain feeling you'll know you've lost." He grinned wide, then spun around to do his handiwork. Rolan had already stood back up, not going down without a fight twirling his two swords, fighting once more.

"Zepa! How can you have let yourself stoop so low?" Rolan then jumped into the air slamming his two swords against his brother who quickly shielded himself.

"Don't lecture me now, brother about my decision! I've made my choice."

He then put out one hand portraying out high winds, pushing Rolan back. The Mandare had landed upon Scar's deck. Telina, who was already close by, rushed over along with Floyd, Scout, and few people. "No Scar!" Telina cried out. While two men helped him off. It then flew back into the air heading back to the battle. "Hurry. We must take care of his wound!" Someone took him below to a room, while others rushed to get the necessary medicine cleaning tools to help him. While Telina waited outside. "Do you think he'll make it?" asked another soldier to another while he walked past his room.

Her eyes became weary. "He'll make it," said Floyd, who swooped between the two soldiers and hovered next to Telina. The man just turned around, still walking, staring at Floyd as he did the same and squinted his three eyes. Then focused his attention on Telina. "Don't worry. Scar's tough. He did get thrown one hundred feet. I'm sure he can survive a knife wound. I'm positive he will survive." While the two waited for Scar to recover, the battle was nearing the end. Rolan and Zepa continued to fight using their powers at full strength of what they had left both dodging fireballs. They impacted everywhere frequently. The two collided once more. While Kanos began to slowly regain consciousness. Zepa then yelled loudly clanging his sword against his brothers wildly like a madman.

He backed his brother almost to an ice wall till he then raised his hands up and created spears that sprouted out from his ice wall. Rolan was so exhausted, he had no escape. Zepa had cornered him against the wall. Rolan's back almost was pricked by a spear. Kanos groaned, rubbed his eyes, and opened them completely. They suddenly grew big. Of what was about to happen, he had to stop it! The two brothers were fighting now for the upper hand both pushing all their might. Rolan turned his head around briefly to his fate. *Clang!* "You're finished, brother. This all could been avoided if you'd just joined us!" Rolan then collapsed to his knees sweating, too tired to move, helpless.

Zepa raised his hand in the air. Wind slowly came, and his brother was pricked by an ice spear just enough to feel the sharp pain singe him slightly. "Brother, I'll give you one more chance. Join, or become one of the dead, like so many before you." Rolan breathed heavily.

"I... I will never join such a cruel force of evil!" Rolan began to slightly tear up. "If this is how I die, then I know I lived my life right." He began to smile and lifted his head up to the sky smiling. Looking at the sun that was finally coming back out to welcome the world despite all the famine and chaos.

"*So be it.*" Zepa's eyes turned white and gray. Then black. Raising both his hands ready to push his brother back fully into the giant ice spears. *Slash!* A loud cry of agony was shot out from Zepa. He slowly turned around feeling his back at the same time that drenched blood. Kanos stood in front of him raising the bloody sword that did its job well smiling. Zepa then squinted his eyes, then shot into the air on currents of wind.

"So you think you've won?" Blood dripped off his back. He then looked around to see that the war seem to have sieged. Every evil force had fallen but him. "You will die, Zepa! It's over. Montorious is dead." Zepa just looked down for a moment.

"So it appears to be to be." He smirked. He flew higher into the air still dripping blood. "See you soon, brothers." At that moment Sabastain and Aaron came rushing over to where their other brothers were. Zepa then took out into the clouds. Loud cheering erupted over the battlefield. Many hugged. Victory was won! Mandare swooped down to carry everyone back to their ships. King Typhus took the lead.

He then told the beast he was upon to land at the castle. "Some of you come with me!" He wanted to make sure that no other creations were hiding. A large group joined Typhus. They landed and charged the back entrance. Kanos and the rest of his friends went to go see him. They saw him asleep and bandaged up. Telina sat by his side. Scout lay at the end of the bed with Floyd.

"Hang in there, old friend," said Sabastain. They all waited patiently hoping he'd pull through. An hour passed but still no luck. They began to fear the worst. "Look!" yelled Kanos. Scar's eyes began to slowly open. He saw Telina sitting on his bed. He reached out his hand and held hers. She leaned down and kissed him.

"I thought I lost you."

"Well, I've been through worse." He smirked. Then turned his head to see familiar faces. He became overjoyed to see that they all survived. Scar tried to sit up.

"Take it easy," said Adam.

"I'm fine. Where's King Typhus?"

"He's fine, just searching the castle with some men to make sure they're all dead."

"Then I should be there also!" Scar arose completely up, then got out of bed.

"No, Scar." Telina grabbed his hand. "Stay. They have it covered."

"No, I want to help." He then went to the corner where his sword was. Then headed to the front door.

"You're so stubborn sometimes." Telina followed behind. Everyone in the room followed Scar to the top deck and rode a Mandare and followed Floyd to the seemingly empty castle. Once they arrived inside, they heard mass yelling ahead.

145

They rushed to where it was coming from passing many rooms, being cautious. Making a left then a right. Then walked into a room where Typhus, Nabeth, Sepada, and some men from all their forces were all arguing among themselves. But became silent once they saw Scar.

"What's going on?" asked Scar. They all just stared in sadness at Scar and his friends. Scar then made a worried expression. Then look around the room to see dozens of posters all over the walls of weird giant machines and other things. "What is this?" asked Scar stepping further into the room. They all made a path for him to where Typhus sat at a desk that was filled with papers. Typhus sighed deeply.

"Scar, you're going to want to take a look at this." Scar swallowed hard and stepped to the desk. Floyd flew onto his shoulder. Then looked down shifting his eyes racing across the entire desk covered in papers.

"*No*," said Scar, covering his face. His friends rushed and gathered around the desk. Telina began to cry for the papers below. Showed numerous sites around the world of places where there were hidden labs. While other papers showed new creations and recent dates. Scar just backed up slowly. "How could we have been so foolish to think that this was the end?" Scar sighed deeply falling to his knees in despair. "For this was just only the beginning of the end and the true wrath of the great Montorious."